THE HIDDEN DEAD

Tracy Whitwell was born, brought up and educated in the North-East of England. She wrote plays and short stories from an early age, then in the nineties moved to London where she became a busy actress on stage and screen.

After having her son, she wound down the acting to concentrate on writing full time. Many projects followed until she finally found the courage to write her first novel, *The Accidental Medium* – a work of fiction based on a whole heap of crazy truth.

Today, Tracy lives in North London with her son, and has written quite a stack of novels. She is nothing like her lead character Tanz in the Accidental Medium series. (This is a lie.)

More by the author

Adventures of an Accidental Medium series

The Accidental Medium

Gin Palace

Cross Bones

THE HIDDEN DEAD

TRACY WHITWELL

PAN BOOKS

First published 2025 by Pan Books
an imprint of Pan Macmillan
The Smithson, 6 Briset Street, London EC1M 5NR
EU representative: Macmillan Publishers Ireland Ltd, 1st Floor,
The Liffey Trust Centre, 117–126 Sheriff Street Upper,
Dublin 1, D01 YC43
Associated companies throughout the world
www.panmacmillan.com

ISBN 978-1-0350-3704-9

1 3 5 7 9 8 6 4 2

A CIP catalogue record for this book is available from the British Library

Typeset in Stempel Garamond by Jouve (UK), Milton Keynes
Printed and bound by CPI Group (UK) Ltd, Croydon, CR0 4YY

For Jack and Kate Deam, soul travellers and Earth warriors both. Love you, my dear friends.

PROLOGUE

'*Chosen.*'

I hear it, crystal clear from within the fog, only a few feet away. That unmistakable timbre. My heart leaps and Thor's expression changes to fearful wonder.

'Tanz . . . ? Did you . . . ?'

I touch his arm. 'Shhhhh . . .'

We both sit in silence and wait. Surrounded by impenetrable mist in the crisp, cold air, it becomes apparent that all birdsong has stopped, everything has stopped. Perfect, unbroken stillness. Then the voice once more.

'*Come.*'

I stand in answer and so does Thor. 'Are you hearing him in Icelandic or English, Thor?'

He whispers back. 'Icelandic. You?'

'English.'

'Fuck.'

I take Thor's hand and lead him to the rowan tree. The plate has gone. So has the pendant.

I put my fingers to my lips and we stand in reverent silence together until he speaks again.

'*With thanks, Chosen and Thor. It is time. Follow.*'

My heart leaps in my chest like a startled rabbit. Thor tightens his grip.

Despite the fog, we can see a shadow ahead. Both of us. We shouldn't be able to see it but we do. It radiates light, but dark light, if that's possible. It moves away from us and a shadowy arm indicates a direction.

'*Follow.*'

Hand in hand, we do as we're told and follow the shadow into the deepest fog.

XIU

ALMOST A WEEK EARLIER

When Sheila and I arrive at the mansion flat in Hampstead, it's already dark outside, even though it's barely 5 p.m. The flat itself is flippin' beautiful. Sheila lives in a fair-sized studio room in Crouch End that's decorated like the inside of a particularly flamboyant gypsy caravan, a style she carries on into her own attire. I have my bigger, but still modest, rented flat up towards Alexandra Palace with a tiny back garden and a looming end-of-contract headache. But *this*? This is the Sistine Chapel of apartments, if the Sistine Chapel had lush cream carpets deeper than Saltwell Park Lake. Bo, who owns the place, is Chinese and I'd say around forty years old, though I can't properly tell as there looks like more than a smattering of Botox going on there. He has close-cropped glossy hair and wears a cashmere roll-neck sweater and very expensive trousers. He smells like heaven in a spicy tobacco and Tuscan leather way and has a perfectly clipped English accent. He gets us both to take off our shoes and leads us through the vaulted hallway into the posh as hell living room, with its cream walls and crimson cushions. Nearby, three separate flames are dancing in a gorgeous wood-and-musk-scented candle that looks to be the size of a window cleaner's bucket, and almost definitely cost as much as last week's rent. My rent, I mean. I can't imagine Bo ever having to pay rent; he's a famous interior designer and has worked for people so rich they've never even seen a Vauxhall Corsa. He doesn't rent things, he buys them.

Sheila, my favourite fifty-something psychic medium, is looking around the place in absolute awe. Bo motions us towards a massive sofa that looks too new to sit on and as we both park ourselves, he nods and settles into a cream leather reading chair. Sheila smiles at him and kicks off the conversation. I always let her start because she's much more experienced in ghost-busting than I am.

'So, what can we do for you, Bo? You said on the phone that some strange things have been happening?'

Bo looks nervous. I've seen him on TV and he doesn't usually look anything but warm and unruffled. He clears his throat.

'First of all, I just have to reiterate, this has to stay a private matter, is that okay? I don't want any of my, erm, fans thinking I've gone mad.'

'Of course, darlin'. We're not blabbermouths, are we, Tanz?'

I smile reassuringly.

'No, of course. We're very discreet.'

I have to work hard not to blink as I say this. Drunk me is the least discreet person on planet earth but I resolve there and then that I'll take this one to my grave.

'So, like I said, things have been moving about. I've lived here two years and until a few months ago it was a peaceful haven. Now it feels . . . well . . . *angry* when I come through the door. And then I'll be sitting watching TV and something will literally move. An ornament or a cup. Not far but enough to creep the hell out of me.'

The TV that Bo is referring to has a huge slimline screen that takes up most of the wall. It must be like being in a cinema when he switches it on. I'm getting serious life-envy right now. I want to live here and watch that telly with a giant glass of vino in my hand. Preferably white because I'd be shit scared of red wine staining the carpet. I wouldn't care about the spooks; I'd ask them to join me but keep quiet. I decide to pipe up again before I swallow my jealous tongue.

'Has anything changed in the past few months, Bo? If it only started recently, it may be that you've annoyed "someone".'

His smooth little face suddenly registers alarm, as much as the Botox will allow.

'Oh, erm . . . not that I can remember. I did put some clutter away when the carpet fitters came. That's all I can think of.'

As he speaks, his clipped vowels almost as sharp as his precise haircut, something catches my attention on the windowsill to the left of Bo. I nudge Sheila, who looks towards the bud vase which is now slowly edging itself forwards. Bo catches my eye and glances behind him just as the crystal trinket launches itself past his head and into the deep-pile carpet at his feet. He yelps, mutters something in his native tongue, then after ten seconds of us all staring at the unharmed vase in wonder, he jumps up and runs towards the kitchen.

'I need a drink!'

I am so impressed with this little display of 'look at me, I'm here' that I burst out laughing and Sheila joins me. I give a tiny round of applause.

'I don't know who you are but that was impressive! Bravo. And you didn't even break anything.'

Sheila squints her eyes then turns to me. 'You see anything?'

'No, just a slight heat haze by the window. Whoever it is isn't very tall. What are you seeing?'

Just then Bo returns with a tray, balancing three of the most beautiful champagne flutes in existence on it, along with a silver bucket containing a pretty fucking expensive bottle of plonk. I nod at him in admiration. This man definitely has the life I'm supposed to be living.

'Bo, Tanz is right. It's a lady, she's not very tall, she looks a bit like you but she's much older and she's got a right face on her. You've pissed her off. She's got . . . Oh, look, she's got a lily in her hair.'

It's all he can do to set the tray down without dropping it when he hears this. I'm primed and ready to lunge and catch the bottle, but luckily everything makes it onto the cream marble table safe and sound. He looks to Sheila in absolute wonder then goes to a Heal's sideboard; I know it's Heal's because I saw the exact same one on his show and was scandalized at how much anyone could charge for something you're probably going to store Sellotape, string and old batteries in. He looks through the bottom drawer and pulls out a framed photo. He hands it to Sheila.

'Is this who you can see?'

It's a black-and-white photo of a lady with an inscrutable face who does indeed look like Bo, with a lily pinned into her hair. I think her eyes are naughty. Sheila nods and gives an impressed whistle.

'This is exactly her, though she's definitely older now. Who is it?'

Bo begins to fill the flutes with fizzy nectar.

'That's my Aunt Xiu. My parents died when I was very young and she brought me up. She made sure I had the best education in Beijing. She was a no-nonsense woman, mostly kind but a bit harsh. I'd always wanted to come to London and so I left her when I was eighteen to go to the Royal College of Art.'

He hands us both a foaming flute.

'She died when I was twenty. I used to write to her but hadn't seen her for nearly two years. I felt so bad.'

I take a sip. It's delicious. 'So why do you think she's pissed off now? It's a long time since she died.'

He sits again.

'I'm not sure but when I had the place revamped, I put her photo in the drawer, and put all the remnants of my childhood up into the loft. They didn't go with the décor, you see. I got some new stuff imported.' He points to an opulent-looking red-and-white mask on the wall. I know it's a Jing mask, from the Chinese opera; we learned about them in drama school.

'I haven't forgotten my past but I like to live in the now. And that might be why she's upset.'

Sheila sips thoughtfully, then cocks her head. I can see a heat haze in the air close to her left ear. She shakes her head at Bo.

'She's saying something about your name, love. Keeps saying "name, name" and pointing at you.'

He exhales sharply and takes a gulp.

'Oh God.'

'She's saying something, I can't quite make it out. Starts with an H.' I can see the shape of a small woman now, next to Sheila. Yes, she has a stern look on her face but she exudes something else. There's another layer to her. It's fascinating. Bo is open-mouthed and waffling, trying to justify himself to the dead Chinese aunt who is whispering purposefully to Sheila. I can tell from here that his perfectly manicured hand is shaking as he pours more champagne.

'My name is really Haruto, but it's such an old-fashioned name and I've always gone as Bo since I arrived in England. So a few months ago I officially changed it by deed poll to Bo. It just made sense . . . I didn't mean to offend Xiu. I mean, she'd been dead a LONG time by then . . .'

'Love, she says her brother named you after a long line of men in the family and her own father's name was Haruto. She was very disappointed when you buried your past. She thinks you should be proud of it.'

Bo bows his head. 'I'm sorry, Auntie.'

I'm actually quite shocked by all of this, as in his TV show he leans pretty heavily on his heritage, but it turns out at home he tries to hide it. Actually, though, that gives me an idea.

'Bo, I know what'll help this. Have you got anything to hand from your childhood? A little thing that ties in with Xiu bringing you up?'

He thinks for a moment then stands.

'There are a few things upstairs. Just a minute.'

He exits and Sheila nods at me.

'She's very upset to be forgotten. Likes you, though.'

'And I like her. Back in a tick.' I scoop up the unbroken little crystal bud vase and pop into the kitchen. There's a huge flower arrangement just by the living-room door so as I walk back with water in the vase, I pluck out a flower and take it over to that ludicrously expensive sideboard. It's starkly empty on there anyway, so Sheila gets up to add the photo of Xiu right in the middle. I sit the vase beside it and slip in the white-and-yellow lily. There are plenty of luscious candles of varying sizes dotted around the place, so I take a small one in a clay pot that's already lit from the mantelpiece and place it on the other side of the photo. It casts a lovely light across Xiu's face. Just then Bo returns and hands Sheila a tiny piece of carved jade. It's a dragon. Bo smiles.

'My aunt gave it to me, said it was my mother's. I didn't put that away, it's always by my bed.'

Sheila nods and places it in front of the photo.

'There you go, love. A bit of a shrine to your aunt. The woman who brought you up and was so proud of you. A woman who deserves to be honoured and not hidden away. You can add whatever you like to it, as an offering. She was sad you wanted to forget her.'

Bo's eyes fill with tears.

'I'm sorry, Auntie. I felt so guilty not seeing you before you died. I think I tried to bury all thoughts of it. I shouldn't have done that. Thank you for everything.'

He puts his hands together in supplication, says something in Chinese, then bows to the picture.

I see the shadow of a little Chinese woman clap her hands together in satisfaction then ruffle Bo's hair, with no effect whatsoever. Sheila grins at me, then at Bo.

'As long as you keep talking to her, I think she'll be all right now.'

Bo sighs with relief. 'Right, well, I for one need more champagne. Will you join me and we can toast my aunt? I need to say thank you.'

It's becoming apparent that Bo rather likes his plonk. A man after my own heart. If I was as successful as he is, my kitchen would be piled up with very expensive alcohol. I'd also have a TV exactly like his.

As more drinks are poured, I see the heat haze move towards me, and suddenly there's a voice in my head. I know she's speaking Chinese but I also simultaneously translate what she's saying in that tinkling yet wise voice.

'*Journey coming. Secrets. Things that are hidden.*'

I hold out my glass to Bo.

Interesting.

NANNA'S LIVING ROOM

Bo was very, very happy with us and, bolstered by a second bottle of extremely nice champers, he handed us an envelope with more cash in it than we would ever dare charge. For good measure he put us in a cab to his favourite cocktail place, the Lady Caroline, which is only fifteen minutes' walk away, but who was going to say no to a taxi?

I bloody *love* it in here. The wallpaper and carpets are exactly the same as photographs of my nanna's flat in the early seventies, the armchairs are also vintage and a bit knackered, the retro music is brilliant and the cocktails are simply off the scale. Backed up by the envelope of cash, Sheila and I have ordered different pricey cocktails to compare. Sheila's has steam coming off it and tastes like a cherry sour. Mine is creamy and reminds me of an eggnog with a shot of sex in it. I need another one. Well, after all that champagne, 'need' is probably pushing it, but flippin' heck it's delicious.

I lean back in my seat and smile at my friend.

'That one was your win, Sheila. You could actually see her.'

'Oh, darling, I may have seen her but she bloody loved you. She felt an affinity with you in some way.'

'How exciting. I love that. And he was so sweet, wasn't he? Though a bit of a bloody fraud on embracing his Chinese heritage all over the telly. It's like he got rid of the real stuff from his past life and replaced it with the Amazon Prime version.'

'Don't underestimate the power of a buggered-up childhood.'

'I know. But still . . . Nice champagne . . . He's got my life, Sheils.'

She laughs, then appraises me from above the rim of her glass.

'You've not said much about Neil recently.'

Neil, my serial-killer-loving policeman sort-of boyfriend from St Albans, is suddenly thrust rudely into my consciousness.

'Oh, mate, not tonight. I'm feeling so happy, and these cocktails are hitting the spot right now.'

'Okay, but until your play was on at the Old Red Lion you were really into him, weren't you?'

'*MegalAdonis.*' A few months ago now, and I bloody loved it. I finally directed a play, my best friend's show no less; and with three lovely actors from a previous terrible show that we thankfully aborted before it got in front of an audience and made idiots of us all. I made very little money from *MegalAdonis*, as bloody expected, but we had a ball. Unfortunately, there was something about Neil coming to see it on the last night and me having to 'look after' him, when all I wanted to do was flit and chat, that caused a clash in our worlds. He'd seen it on the first night and held my left hand, while Milo, the writer and my best mate, sat on the other side and held my right one, and it had been sweet. Those two had had nice chats and all was right with the world. But after that final night, when I felt a bit trapped, my ardour suddenly cooled. I'd fought to keep things going, as he's such a lovely person and I thought maybe I was just a bit down after the mad time I'd had at the Cross Bones Graveyard, but I've only really seen him once a fortnight since, and last night I told him over the phone that I wanted to take a proper break to 'reassess'. He sounded crestfallen and I felt really bloody guilty. Trust Sheila to pick up on it. I explain it all to her over another drink, while seventies bangers ring out from the jukebox.

'What a shame, Tanz, I liked him. And I mean, many actors' partners aren't in the business. Maybe it's a good balance.'

'Yeah, maybe. But right now, I'm not sure. I feel very confused, and I don't want to hurt him any more than I have to.'

She nods. 'Well, as long as you know what you're doing.'

'As if I ever know what I'm doing.'

As I say this, her eyes rise to a spot behind me and I turn to see a very tall man with shoulder-length wavy hair. He has a double chin and a rather plump belly, is in the kind of flowing shirt you'd see Lord Byron sporting, and is about to put two drinks down on our table. They're a repeat of the cocktails we're already drinking and he's smiling broadly.

'Sorry, ladies, I was sitting over there with my friend and I couldn't help noticing the incredible women with the beautiful auras. I had to bring you over another drink.'

I glance to where he's pointing and see a younger, shy-looking soul with a pint in front of him and perfectly shiny, straight, long dark hair. His skin looks like alabaster from here. He's simply beautiful. They actually look like a pair of ill-disguised father/son vampires and I'm disgusted by my immediate attraction to them. The one standing next to me, who seems extraordinarily confident considering he's the less beautifully maned, much older version of his friend, twinkles at me, and I notice the green tint in his eyes. He leans towards me and sniffs audibly.

'You smell incredible.'

Fuck me, maybe he's an actual *vampire.* I nod, attempting to seem unruffled, glad I wore my new perfume tonight.

'Thank you. What's your accent? I don't recognize it.'

'Oh, sorry, of course, introductions. My name is Einar and I'm Icelandic. My friend over there is Julio, he's Spanish. And you?'

He has a way of looking at you like no one else exists. But more than that, the energy that comes from him is indescribable. Plus, he's a fucking giant. It's actually all so overpowering I'm finding it hard to breathe properly.

'I'm Tanz, I'm a Geordie. And this is Sheila. We've just been working, so this is our wind-down.'

'So what do you do, ladies?'

Sheila half smiles at him. 'We're a pair of witches, sweetheart, so best be careful.'

He throws his head back and emits a hearty guffaw. 'My kind of women!'

He then crinkles his eyes at me and begins to move off. 'Enjoy your evening, northern witch.'

For a fleeting second I wonder if he's spiked the drinks. Then it occurs to me that he was rather too loud and expansive to have drugged our cocktails, as everyone in the bar would know he'd done it. Sheila and I both lift our drinks to him, and he and his friend do the same with their almost-empty glasses. Then we turn away, and Sheila shakes her head.

'Watch him, love. Far too cocky for his own good.'

'You reckon?'

'Of course I reckon. He's nowhere near your league but he thinks he's six tiers above it. He's also got a lot of charisma. Old-school charm. They're the bloody worst.'

I start to giggle, then she joins in. I steal a glance at Einar and he's watching us, also laughing, unaware that he's the cause of our mirth.

'I think he's sexy. He's so tall and frazzled round the edges. He looks like he's lived.'

'What, like a frayed rug that needs throwing out has lived?'

'Wow, Sheila. Talk about brutal.'

She grins at me, the drink now fuzzying her face. 'Just looking out for my mate.'

'Aw, aren't you sweet?'

Her eyes dart up again and suddenly there is Einar once more, teeth glinting at us. The silent, beautiful one is standing behind him, slipping a black leather jacket over his shoulders. Einar offers a small piece of folded, lined paper.

'I have to go now. But your energy is astounding. I would love to talk to you about anything and everything before I leave the country, so here you are.'

He drops the paper in my hand, smiles at both of us, then exits with his friend, who gives a tiny shy smile as he closes the door behind him. I open up the paper. It's a phone number and the words *We were meant to meet.*

I show Sheila and she shakes her head. 'What a dickhead. I'd throw that bloody thing in the bin.'

I fold the paper twice more, into the tiniest square, then slip it into the back of my purse. I'm far too intrigued to throw it. What a strange, interesting man.

HOODOO FUNK

I'm very restive when I get home and not as drunk as I thought I'd be, which is probably because of the sugar in tonight's drinks, plus all of the evening's shenanigans, ghostly and not so ghostly. So I elect to put on a film, cuddle my sleek, black, feline right-hand woman, Inka, and try to forget about the text I just received from Neil, expressing no wish to pressure me but saying he just wanted to let me know he still thinks I'm 'amazing'.

With the lamps and candles lit and a peppermint tea in front of me, I begin to slip comfortably out of consciousness in front of the TV, head lolling to the side, as Inka snuggles on my lap, purring like an idling combine harvester. Just as I'm winking out completely I could swear I hear Frank, my dead but definitely not departed Geordie mate, whisper something in my ear. It sounds like 'Hoodoo Funk'. *What the bloody hell is 'Hoodoo Funk', Frank, you weirdo?* As expected, I hear nothing else. He's hit and run as per. But next thing I know, I'm not in my living room any more.

Suddenly I'm standing near a cliff edge at night. The sky is amazingly clear but I have no idea where I am and it's bloody freezing. There's a man lurking right by the drop; he's bearded, probably a little older than me, and wearing what looks like a massive fisherman's jumper. He's staring over the edge with a blank look on his face, not moving a muscle. I wonder what he's feeling, but all at once get a strong sense that I really don't want to go there; he has secrets and hidden depths that aren't pleasant. I just hope he's not about to kill himself. I'm aware that I'm in a dream, but dream or not, I don't want to witness a suicide. Just then I catch a movement from the corner of my eye, and about twenty feet away a shadow emerges from behind some scrubby bushes. I can't see a face on the shadow-person shape, just long hair and a tall build. This one's interesting because I'm fucking frozen while wearing what feels like a big fat cardigan and boots, but they seem to just be wearing trousers and a long shirt of some kind. For reasons I also can't fathom, I have no sense of the sex or intention of this figure; they're made of shadow and mystery, which is partly scary and partly exciting. As I stand here, feeling my fingertips go numb, there's a noise. A note from a horn – a giant horn made of bone is what I feel – which starts low and quiet, but quickly builds. It's deep and melancholic and extremely magical. Goosebumps begin to spring up on my arms as the note continues to sound, then I gasp as the head of the shadowy figure moves, and suddenly I see eyes made of light that matches the stars above me, boring straight into my soul. And at that moment I'm so scared, I leg it.

In the real world, what that means is I wake up with a huge start that sees my legs kicking into the air and Inka letting out a frightened squeak as she launches herself out of the room, leaving a bunch of very impressive punctures in the skin above my knee. The scratches quickly produce blood and I hurry to the bathroom to get some raw TCP on a cotton ball; TCP is the cure-all in my universe and I welcome the sting. I don't blame Inka for this, incidentally. She rarely exposes her claws so I must have really scared her. Once I'm done, I put a plaster over the cuts, then go to the kitchen to get a glass of wine for me and a cat treat for Inka. She'll not hide under my bed for long, and will expect compensation for what happened on her return.

Back in the living room I put on some soothing music and shout out for Frank with my mind. He doesn't answer, the bugger, so I'll have to ask him later. I'm not oblivious to the fact that the shadowy man in my dream had long hair, just like those attractive vampires we met in the bar. Maybe what I just saw was connected to that, especially considering my rather extreme reaction to that Einar fella. I actually got breathless around him. Sheila was right, he was cocky, but he was also twinkly and unfathomable and had intriguing eyes. His weightiness, which made me think he must love his booze and his food, just added to the allure. I've never snogged such a big lad before and it's very bad that I'm thinking about him like this, because it means I'm already moving on from Neil and he's done absolutely nothing wrong. Maybe I'm just bloody nuts. Don't narcissists go off people in the blink of an eye? Am I a fucking narcissist now?

I dig the square of paper from the deepest recesses of my purse and unfold it. It's no big deal if I save the number in my phone, is it? I mean, it doesn't mean I'll message him. I type in his name and the digits and press 'save'. I have absolutely no intention of saying anything to him, so am as surprised as anybody when I find myself typing the words . . .

Nice to meet you, Einar. Thank you for the drink.

The reply comes back scandalously quickly.

Thank you for smelling incredible and filling the whole room with light. Come to dinner tomorrow.

Of course I'm not going to dinner with him tomorrow. That would be madness.

VIVA LA REVOLUCIÓN!

I am absolutely bricking it. I shouldn't be here. I mean, I haven't 'technically' completely broken up with Neil, have I? I'm just getting some 'space'. It's a gorgeous old pub called The Holly Bush, all wood and leather and expensive matt paint. My heart's pounding and my hands are clammy as I stand at the bar, and the way my knees are shaking it becomes evident that if I don't sit down in a minute, I may faint. Just then Einar comes through the door and his smile makes all the wall lamps brighter. The place is pretty full, but he seems to have swung what is, in my opinion, the prime spot. It's a small round table with two seats opposite each other, right in front of the pub's open fire, which has a fire guard in front of it – probably a good idea while I'm feeling so faint.

He pulls out my seat for me, then perches on the other, everything in this world obviously too small for him. Hanging his jacket over the back of his chair, he reveals a fitted black shirt and black jeans, with a large silver ankh around his neck. I can see a little of his chest and it's mostly hairless and smooth. I try not to stare but he notices.

'The ankh. Egyptian sign for life. I am a devotee of living life to its fullest. How about you?'

'Well, I'm here, aren't I, so I'm not dead yet.'

'That's not what I meant. What would you like to drink? You like champagne?'

I laugh, trying to sound earthy and not shrill. 'Of course.'

He waves to a barman, who comes over with menus and winks at Einar, who must have been here before.

'What can I do for you, my Viking friend?'

'Bottle of the Perrier-Jouët, please, while we look at the menus.'

I love Perrier-Jouët. I smile at him as he hands me the menu.

'I do love life, Einar. But it's not easy to feel carefree all the time. There's always something to worry about.'

He nods. 'Worries are always hanging about, Tanz, but we can live like kings anyway. Be free!'

There is something about this man. He's huge and full of enthusiasm and his accent is so interesting. Also, the timbre of his voice is deeply lyrical. It seems to resonate in the centre of my soul. That said, he's also a bit full of himself and if I don't bear that in mind, I will surely regret it. I know this is lust for me, and I'm a bloody nightmare when I really fancy someone. He does have a delectable mouth, though, and it's making my senses prickle. I stare at the menu to try to stop myself from watching his lips. He has a cupid's bow, which is very pink and young-looking, contrasting with the thinning shoulder-length hair and the drinker's nose, which is a strong shape but definitely has the thread veins of a man who likes a lot of booze. As a shallow actress this would usually put me off, but with him, no, not at all. He's a true character. And now I'm beginning to wonder how his skin smells. *Shit.*

I spot Padrón peppers on the menu. I know I won't be able to eat a proper meal in front of this one-off man, so I suggest a bowl of those to share and put my menu down. He calls the waiter again and orders my peppers, plus a bunch of other tapas-type dishes we can pick at. Nothing too heavy. The champagne arrives almost immediately and Einar fills our flutes to the top, eyes glinting as the froth doesn't quite overbrim. This man tips the glasses. He 'knows'.

'*Salute.*'

'*Salute* to you. Good champagne choice.'

He narrows his eyes at me, like he's wondering what I think of him.

'I hope that wasn't presumptuous; I feel like I know you. A witch and a wizard in the same room. We're lucky all the electricity doesn't blow.'

'You're a silver-tongued sod, aren't you?'

'Many good things have been said about my tongue. Silver or not.'

My cheeks grow hot. He truly couldn't give a fuck what he says and yes, he rather fancies himself and his intensity should be a red flag the size of a W7 bus, but frankly, I don't care in the slightest.

'So how come you think you're a wizard then?'

'Magic. There's magic everywhere in Iceland. I feel it, and I hone it. I make things happen for myself, and for others, and the energy from it helps me live my life to the absolute maximum. There is no point being timid about who you are and what you want. We're here for the blink of an eye. And as for magic, who fucking cares if some people don't believe in it. They miss out and we benefit.'

'I don't think of magic as a way to power, you bloody heathen. It's there to *help* others.'

'Of course it is, but you are a person too. You also have to help yourself.'

I'm pretty sure Fagin sings a song about that in *Oliver*. I actually find Einar's honesty refreshing. If he was some cockney estate agent, maybe not, but his accent and veneer of glamour make me giddy.

As I sip more, he tells me about his life in Iceland (he's here on business with his computer firm) and I get the strongest feeling I've known him for ever. Of course, I sound like a wanker saying this, but it's true, it's not just him feeling that connection; his energy is contagious. Within a very short time I'm laughing my head off. We nibble at the small plates of food but mostly we drink and we chat. I've never met anyone from Iceland before; his voice lulls me, and when he laughs he looks like a naughty schoolboy. He says he loves his job and the travel that goes with it. People in England never really admit to loving anything. They 'like' things, they sort-of enjoy things. They never seem to devour life like it's a giant, greasy goose leg, as he does. After food we graduate to a leather banquette. Suddenly I'm sitting close to him, and his cheeky smile actually makes me feel rather feral. I can smell him now. Warmth radiates from him, amplifying his clean hair.

'Are you wearing aftershave?'

He winks. 'Aha. Yes, it's a unisex scent that you can only get from Reykjavík. Subtle but effective. You like?'

I'm fighting the urge to bite his neck, he smells so good. 'Yes, it's quite . . . effective . . .'

He laughs, leans forward, then leans back again.

'Oops. I nearly kissed you then,' he says.

Please don't judge me, I'm feeling rather squiffy now and I beam at him.

'Oh dear. Maybe I should kiss you first, then you won't feel so bad.'

He looks surprised and not displeased as I lean forward and touch my lips to that irresistible cupid's bow. His kiss is as soft as any I've ever experienced, but it feels like there's something behind it. Something huge and unquantifiable. The rush I feel as I taste his tongue is, to put it mildly, 'unladylike'. We break off for a few seconds, then I kiss him again and, worried that I might actually lose control here in front of everyone, I lean away and take a sip from my drink. When I look back at him, he stares searchingly into my eyes, and his serious face makes me laugh. Then he gets up and goes to the bar, returning moments later and handing me my coat.

'Come.'

I leave the rest of my drink and stand. He's obviously paid. I slip on my jacket like a good little girl and as we leave the bar, he takes my hand and leads me along the road.

'Let me show you where I'm staying. When you virtually run the company, they treat you right. Plus, I have wine. Good wine!'

He suddenly stops, leans forward and this time he kisses me. My arms don't even stretch the whole way round him as I hold him and the kiss goes on far longer than is decent in public. The rest of the walk is a short blur before we're entering a flat, the whole first floor of a house that's down a pretty, quiet side street. Inside it's all dark blue, black and gold. Opulent but also comfy. Not as gobsmackingly big as Bo's place, but certainly lovely, and I'd probably give a couple of my less important toes to live here.

As soon as we're in the living room, he lights lamps and candles. There's one particular lamp which is a crow holding a lightbulb that I covet and make a note of as something I'm determined to own. Then I sit back on the large black velvet couch as Einar places two glasses on the low table before us and pours from a very cold bottle of Sancerre. He then presses a button that fills the room with music, the kind of old blues that makes you want to drink bourbon and smoke a cigar, though of course I'd vomit if I actually did that. Instead, I raise my glass to Einar, who has now sat himself closer than he has to on such a big sofa. Two sips in and he takes my glass from me and puts that cupid's bow against my lips once more. The electric shock is something else. I have this strange buzzing in the middle of my brain, sexy bees or maybe horny wasps, and my stomach has melted. The kiss gets deeper and then he moves back and pulls his shirt over his head. His chest is wide and smooth with a tiny smattering of hairs and of course the ankh, and his face is a mask of impishness. He has everything but my underwear off me in thirty seconds flat. In his boxers, he does look like some gigantic Norse god who got dumped on earth and is just too expansive for this small world, but he's also surprisingly graceful. He deftly manoeuvres me so I'm straddling him, and kisses me like I'm his next meal. Then suddenly a song comes on that I've always loved, something I heard my dad play when I was little, and I throw my arm in the air.

'CHOON!'

Next thing I know I've been pulled up and am dancing on an expensive-looking rug with a man who has chucked his boxers in the air and is now stark bollock naked. I try not to look but can't help it, and I discover that this huge man is thoroughly in proportion. Throwing caution (and underwear) to the corner of the room, I join him, and we dance naked like a pair of children to the rolling beat, singing along and not thinking about how we look. *I never, ever don't think about how I look. And certainly not when I'm naked.* At the end of the song, we entwine on the sofa again and drink our wine, kissing and talking. It's extraordinary. The weird thing is, we heavy pet endlessly but never actually have sex. To my joy, he understands books and art, so we chatter away, and by the time I jump in a cab at 4 a.m., safe in the knowledge that I didn't sleep over or have actual sex, so I'm really a good girl and not going to hell, I know that I'm more than a little besotted. I feel utterly alive. Before I'm even in my own bed, still cleaning my teeth as the birds begin their chorus outside, I receive a text from Einar.

I'm flying back to Iceland tomorrow. If you seriously want to escape, jump on a plane and stay in my summer house. You can kick back and do some writing.

Okay, so I told him I wanted to write and direct my own stuff as I've gone off acting, in between juicy kisses and losing my mind with lust. But I can't just fly to a country I don't know and meet up with someone I've just met. Someone who made my thighs into the Niagara Falls but didn't actually shag me. Fucking hell, how am I going to stop thinking about him? He's brought out my crazy. I'm lost over a man who spouts outrageous compliments like confetti and also tells me what to do. I'd usually slap a bloke who did that.

'He's such a douche.'

I put my toothbrush down. 'Frank?'

Frank almost never pops up when I ask him to these days, but then he'll randomly start saying things in my head when I least expect it, and he has a strong opinion on everything. We never got together before he died, but he still seems to think he has the right to vet every bloke I meet. Virtually no one meets his standards.

'Really, Tanz, your taste is getting worse, not better.'

I sit on the edge of the bath.

'Frank, he's rocked my world. What do I do?'

'*You know, sometimes it's like babysitting a polecat! Why are your choices so awful? What about your policeman?*'

'Fucking hell, leave Neil out of this. Why is everyone so obsessed with Neil? And YOU are the man who led me into a knife attack from a homicidal nutter. I could have died. That was quite a messed-up choice.'

'*I made sure you were okay. Anyway, you love adventures.*'

'Not ones that lead to my immediate demise.'

'*Fancying twats will lead to your mind's demise.*'

'He just gave me the best night ever! Why does that make him a twat, you jealous swine?'

'*Oh, so I'm jealous now? Find out for yourself, you flippin' stubborn cow. Anyway, forget him, he's not the main story. You've got a proper adventure coming up.*'

My heart lurches. Frank announcing things like this always leads to something wonky happening. Usually involving spookiness and danger.

'Well, I'm off on a little holiday on my own for a few days. I can do without a huge drama while I'm there, so wait until I'm back before unleashing this next "adventure" on me, okay?'

'*You're actually GOING?*'

'Why the hell not?'

I hear that familiar laugh. '*Okay, you loon. Do what you must.*'

'I bloody will.'

I seem to have just told Frank I'm going to Iceland. Even thinking of it makes my insides jump; the absolute rebelliousness of it sends my heart soaring. What the hell is with this Einar bloke? It's like I chucked out paracetamol and Night Nurse, and jumped head first into crystal meth as my favourite medicine. But reason be damned, if I can go somewhere new for a bit, and get a fresh viewpoint on where my life's headed, what's the harm? Life's for living, isn't it? Even if it turns out to be a disaster, it's just a few days and it'll be something to tell someone else's grandkids. (Not mine, I'm pretty sure that horse has bolted.)

Viva la Revolución! Or something . . .

SANE?

I cannot believe I'm on a plane to Keflavík. When I got to Luton airport this morning it was 5.40 a.m. and the quietest I've ever seen an airport in my life, probably because it still wasn't 'next day' yet. Because I'm an idiot my 'early night' last night turned into three double gin and tonics, while I cuddled Inka and listened as my best mate Milo yapped down the phone at me 'til midnight. It started off about how ridiculous I was to be flying out to a country I'd never visited before to meet a man I'd only realistically known for two days, then how much he liked Neil, but later moved on to other important subjects like 'do ghosts ever get worried?' and 'can you really take a man seriously if he wears chinos in primary colours?'. (Answers: probably not unless that ghost died worried, and no.)

Right now, as I wave away the chance of a plastic cup of weak granulated coffee from a nice air hostess, I'm remembering the last time I was on a plane. I was off to shoot an advert in Spain, and my deceased friend Frank visited me in a dream on my flight to let me know he'd never 'gone' anywhere, was always with me, and I was about to embark on quite the adventure. Well, he wasn't fucking wrong and it's not stopped since. Mysteries, countless ghosts, and far too much bloody danger. Twice I've nearly been murdered. TWICE. I need this holiday, I need a reset, that's how I'm justifying this impetuous act.

It has definitely occurred to me that I 'may' be having an existential crisis. I've had a few and this big one has been pressing in for quite a while now, ever since my acting career began to truly lose its lustre, in fact. By the time you've done a few ghost-busts, been in mortal danger more than once and had a beautiful old soul die in your arms, pretending to be other people in sub-par productions starts to feel more and more preposterous. I don't know who I am any more, but the thing about existential crises is that running away is a great way to divert the anxiety. And running away to a man that turns you into a snarling cavewoman when you remember him naked, to the extent you can't think about anything else, is simply too tempting. Especially when you've done several voiceovers in the past few months and can actually afford to take a tiny break. Maybe I've finally gone properly mad. Or maybe I've woken up and become sane at last.

'*I doubt you ever have been or ever will be sane in your whole life.*'

'Oh, hello, Frank. Thought you'd show your face, did you?'

'*Of course. We have history when it comes to planes.*'

'I know we do. Happy aeroplane anniversary. Good you popped up right now, I'm just thinking about how intense everything's been. I reckon I might have PTSD after all the shenanigans in Southwark. I needed to get away from London to process it all, so this is perfect.'

Ever since the drama at Cross Bones Graveyard and my brush with another murderer, there's been something jumpy in me. While I was directing my friends in *Megal-Adonis*, I was able to bury myself in work and drinking with Gerald, who has now officially become my London actor BFF. But since then I've been 'staying in' much more than I used to. Apart from making a crust from a few voiceovers, then the ghost-bust at Bo's with Sheila, I've been hiding, my social life conducted by phone.

'So much PTSD, you were at a strange man's abode the other night having a blast.'

I'm not always truly serious with Frank, but right now I go for it.

'Frank, that night took a lot of courage. I went by cab because I didn't want to get the tube alone. Then drink and Einar's company relaxed me. He's huge and clever and being around him made me feel protected. As for the debauchery, sex is another way to hide, another way to escape, isn't it? And now I'm absolutely gaga over him already. I don't trust myself any more. I need to change "things", but what things? Where do I start?'

I feel a warm rush of air against my face, and a shot of energy at the back of my neck that immediately dissipates again. I twitch slightly and look around me, wondering if anyone else felt it. There's a woman next to me who must be late sixties with a grey pixie cut and a vast amount of blue eyeshadow. She's fast asleep with ear protectors on, so I won't be getting any replies from her.

'Don't worry, Tanz, that's Jemima you just felt. You're getting a healing right now. I know I took the piss about you flying to Iceland but actually you do need this. Just not for the reasons you think. It'll open your eyes. And everything always becomes clear in the end, doesn't it?'

Actually it bloody doesn't, but I'm not going to argue too hard about it, as I suddenly feel a lot more relaxed. Jemima is a 'being' who started helping me when I was up to my eyes in the 'Creepy Dan the Creepy Murderer' saga. Jemima is a tall, blue, glowing angel. I have to be careful who I talk to about these things, as seeing blue angels can get you put away.

'I'm hoping to write something when I'm out there, you know. It's not just a desperate dash to get another snog from Einar.'

'The reasons you're going don't matter. If you're meant to be somewhere, then just go with the flow and see what happens.'

'I will. And I promise you, it does feel like the right thing. Iceland feels like it's calling me. Just tell me I'm not flying into the arms of a fucking nut-job murderer.'

'I'm telling you no such thing. It keeps things fun.'

Even as a ghost, Frank is one twisted boy.

'God, you're impossible.'

'Rightbackatcha.'

DRUMBEAT IN MY GUT

This airport is lovely. Roomy and not overcrowded. I'm feeling all weird again. I'll be seeing Einar soon and I'm shaking with nerves. Am I meant to be this lost over someone I just met? I think part of the excitement is that he makes me feel impetuous. I danced naked with him as soon as he got me alone, and I've jumped on a plane to his home country the same week I met him. As I walk the corridor towards the exit, which is apparently through a supermarket where you can get booze and essentials more cheaply than in town, I pass a cabinet filled with the strangest curiosities. Taxidermy no less. Taxidermy alongside goods made of animal skin. But the strangest curiosity of all is that it's going on 10 a.m. and the sun is only just rising outside. At this time of year it's only light around seven hours a day and each window I pass shows a dawn that happened two hours earlier in London. Apparently next month there'll only be five hours' light a day, which is crazy. It'll be dark until 11 a.m. and get dark again around 4 p.m. It's bloody otherworldly.

I buy champagne that I can't afford but fuck it, a bottle of good red, a Diet Coke and some bits of food, plus a massive bag of chocolates to take with me, because I'm on holiday, right? I'm allowed to let loose a bit.

Outside it's bloody freezing. I brought my 'warm, practical parka', as instructed by Google, and I pull up the hood as I look around at the small car park and the parking place at the side for coaches. Einar already told me he'd be working this morning so I booked one of the coaches into town. It turned out a taxi from here to Reykjavík would be well over a hundred quid, and considering the actual flights here were cheaper than that, I of course quickly discounted that option. The coaches take you to a meeting place and then you're transferred to a smaller bus that drops you at your hotel anyway, so it's pretty much like a taxi service. Though Einar said I could have his summer house outside town for free for three days, I didn't want to take the piss and ask to stay with him in town first, so I've booked an apart-hotel for my first night in the main part of Reykjavík.

There's a man standing at a coach door who's small, blond and smiley and wearing a coat not unlike mine. He checks my ticket and nods, then I clamber up into what is a rather luxurious, new-smelling coach. There are only a handful of people on here, dotted about, mostly with woolly hats on, and I sit near the front. It doesn't take long before we pull off, the coach only about half full, and then as we get onto the road, surrounded by scrubby greenery, I get the funniest feeling in my gut. Below the other feeling of warm, liquid excitement at seeing Einar again, there's the pull of something visceral. This place is an alien landscape to me: no trees that I can see, mostly rocky and mossy with strong-looking bushes. It's a fifty-minute drive and this feeling of an ancient drumbeat in the bottom of my gut continues as the coach moves along, with the sea to the left of us. I wish I could ask questions, especially when I suddenly see the harbour and Reykjavík town in the distance. It's stunning. I can't believe I've not been here before; it feels darkly familiar. I'm very aware that I've basically run off from my own mind. Left London with very little notice so I can stop thinking; didn't even tell Sheila I was going, or my little mam in case she talked me out of going. Obviously I didn't tell Neil either. What the hell would I say? No, only Milo, my cat-sitter and my acting agency know I'm here. It's my thing. I know how mad it sounds, but I just had to come.

A text arrives from Einar.

See you at your hotel in two hours.

LAUGAVEGUR

The little bus to where I'm staying is cute and I get to see bits of the town as we go from place to place. I love that the houses are all different colours and shapes. Mostly they seem to be clad in corrugated iron, which I thought would make them cold, but obviously not. The buildings are so pretty. The place I'm staying is called 'A Room With A View' and we have to drive onto Laugavegur, which is the main street running through Reykjavík town centre. I looked up the meaning of it, I'm nosy like that, and it means 'wash road', as it used to lead to the hot springs in Laugardalur where in olden times the women of Reykjavík took their laundry for washing. Apparently there are hot springs all over the place in Iceland. It's so exciting how different it is. The driver is very chatty, and he's around my age with a tawny beard. There are a lot of beards here, many blokes walking around with different lengths and designs of facial hair. When he smiles at me there's a dimple in one cheek and his eyes are bright. His voice is lighter than Einar's but still melodic and gentle.

'The water here comes from springs under the earth. Cold water from the tap is as pure as anything you'd get in a bottle, more pure, and the hot water is ready heated from hot springs. It smells of sulphur.'

'Wow, like eggs?'

'Yes, like eggs.'

His laugh is infectious. Two elderly American tourists behind me begin to laugh too. The man is in a giant cagoule, even though it's not raining, and wears an insulated hat with fake-fur lining.

'The first time I smelled that water I thought it was off, didn't I, June? I was gonna complain! Then I spoke to this guy at breakfast and he let me know what was what before I made a goddamn fool of myself.'

His wife nods. She's in a green padded coat and a bobble hat.

'He's always making a fool of himself. Lucky he makes good coffee!'

They both laugh more. They're very loud compared to the driver, who's called Thor, pronounced 'Tor'. He points to a parked coach with writing on the side.

'There's a tourist office by the harbour,' he tells me. 'You can book trips to the Golden Circle and get tickets for whale-watching boats. Sometimes if you just stand and wait, you'll see whale pods in the bay and not even have to go out in the boats. Will you be on your own here?'

I'm not sure how to word my reply so I go for the basics.

'Oh, I'm meeting a friend who's showing me around and letting me stay at his summer house, as a bit of a writing retreat.'

He glances thoughtfully at me then nods.

'Nice plan. Well, I'm sure he'll show you some great bars later. There are plenty.'

His English is so good. I have the British shame of only just being able to stumble around conversational French, while in other countries they speak my language better than I do. When he stops outside the hotel, he has to point out the door, it's so well hidden among everything else on the stretch of high street. He writes something down and hands it to me.

'My number. If you need to know anything about tours, about bars, about where to buy good bread, about getting a cab, anything, you give me a call and I can tell you.'

Flippin' heck, do all Icelandic fellas just hand you their number the first time you meet them? Saying that, there doesn't seem to be a trace of lecherousness from this lad as he does it. Warm, friendly and kind. That's Thor. What a fucking sweetheart.

'Thank you. I think I'll be fine but that's very kind.'

He nods and I take my little wheelie case to the door. He drives off and waves to me. The Americans also wave.

So that's it. I'm here.

BUCKING BRONCO

I love my little room-cum-apartment. It has a kitchen, a half-screened-off bedroom bit and a private bathroom. It also has a small balcony, and to the left, over patios and a bit of road, I can see a bar painted in bright colours. It's called Bravo. I like that it looks dark through the windows, like one of the cave-like places I used to go to when I was a fully fledged Goth in my late teens. I've brought a tiny-sized version of my current favourite mentholated shower gel and decide to have a quick freshen up. I have that slightly dizzy feeling you get when you've been up since fuck off o'clock and I reckon a shower with very hot water then a strong coffee should help me back to life before I meet Einar in forty-five minutes. God, I feel crackers when I think of him. That tingle you get when you've broken the rules.

The water, as described, smells of farty eggs, but not enough to put me off. It's so lovely to lather up and be in the heat and steam. Once I'm dried and in my best skinny jeans and warm but well-shaped sweater combo, I make sure my face is in order, comb my hair and make a coffee in the percolator. Luckily the last person here left a half-used bag of real coffee in the cupboard it seems, and the cleaners didn't nab it. I didn't even think to buy coffee. I have it black and it tastes good. I team it with a couple of the chocolates I bought, and the sugar rush is welcome. Another text comes in and it's Einar.

Should I come up or meet you at reception?

Come up. Room 7.

See you in five minutes.

Oh HELL, I should have met him in reception but I'm already on fire just knowing he's in the vicinity. I quickly clean my teeth and very soon there's a knock. The whole door frame is filled with him when I open up. I step back and in he stomps, carrying a bottle of champagne.

'Welcome to Iceland, you mad northerner!'

I take him in. I've spent two days with him in my head as a gigantic, perfect Norse god. Now here he is in slightly knackered black jeans, black shirt which is straining around his middle, large padded jacket, dirty boots, veins on his nose, fine shoulder-length mousy grey hair, unkempt and defo showing scalp, and I have *never* fancied anyone more in my whole life. He leans forward to give me a peck on the mouth and I have to steady myself. He slips his coat onto a hook on the door and pops the champagne cork within seconds, filling two wine glasses to the brim. This is not the way to have champagne. Where are the flutes? Plus, there's no way I should have any when the only food I've had in hours is a couple of chocolates, but I take a large glug anyway then put down my glass.

'Come here.'

He raises an eyebrow then places his own glass, already half empty, by the sink. I hardly let him walk a step before I'm dragging him onto the sofa so our faces are at the same level and I can kiss him feverishly. I sense a bit of resistance, I think he likes to be in control, but I have no time for that right now. I've just flown for two hours fifty minutes and taken a long bus ride, simply so I can smell his skin again. Anyway, once we're there and I'm unbuttoning his shirt buttons like a pro, he seems to catch the bug and virtually carries me to the bed, where all clothes disappear and very soon I'm riding him like a fairground bucking bronco. I don't even know who I am any more, as I shout the place down with abandonment, and then in what seems like a blink, we're side by side, absolutely drenched in sweat and laughing like maniacs. When he's caught his breath, which takes a little while, he goes to grab the two glasses and comes back with them brimming again.

There are little tables with lamps at either side of the bed and I sip my cold fizz then put it down on my one. I lie on my side and watch as he takes in almost a half-glass again in one gulp. This lad really can drink.

'Hello, Einar.' I trace a finger down his chest. 'Nice to see you again.'

He emits a very throaty laugh.

'Nice to see you too. You seemed a little hungry when I arrived. Better now?'

'Yes, thank you. I reckon you've rendered me insane. This is not how I conduct myself on a regular basis.'

'Well then, I'm honoured. As I said to you, always live life to its fullest.'

He salutes me with his glass, drains the rest, then refills it with the dregs of the bottle. Thank goodness I bought another one.

'How was your flight?'

'It was much shorter than I imagined. I don't know where I thought Iceland was but I certainly expected at least four hours on a plane.'

'No, easy commute. Visiting each other is like driving from London to Sheffield or something.'

'Bloody hell. You know England better than I do.'

'Ha. I've done business there a lot. And I'm hoping to get to know it even more intimately now.'

He smiles at me and I feel the prickle of a need for 'round two' coming on. But I also feel something else. The shadow of a trace of a doubt. I smile into his eyes, a paleness to the green, hidden depths beneath, and fight to make it go away. I always doubt that men care about me. I always think they'll hurt me somehow. I'm pretty sure I'm feeling doubt because I really bloody like him. Also, I've been awake since 3.30 this morning. My blood sugar must have plummeted; I really should eat something.

'So, Tanz, there are only a few hours of daylight left, would you like to see something of the place? Then we can grab drinks and I'll drive you to the summer house first thing tomorrow.'

I'd be just as happy mauling him here, with a takeaway for sustenance, but that's crazy of me. I'm in a whole new world. I have to go out and see at least a teensy bit of Einar's homeland.

'Okay. I'm loath to put clothes back on, but come on.'

ESJA

As soon as we're on the street I feel it again. Like a pulse, a drum, a heartbeat, but in my gut, beneath all other feeling. They say that our belly is our second brain, plus the place where we keep all emotions past and present. My emotions are on fire. I'm ready to laugh and cry and jump thirty feet in the air. It's cold and the sky is grey and blue. I can see Bravo bar from the front now, and I love the colours it's been painted. They look vibrant and alive. It's like I'm on drugs. Opposite is a coffee bar that looks like a wooden lodge with a pointy roof and Einar takes me straight over. He nods to the young lass serving, who seems to know him and nods back.

He points at me. 'My friend here needs a cappuccino and a croissant, please, before she faints from hunger. I'll have a black double espresso.' He pays immediately and we sit in the window.

'Hope you don't mind, you were a bit tipsy the other night and said you needed a cappuccino to wake you up. I just assumed that's your preferred coffee.'

I like that he remembers. I'm not usually happy when people order for me, but I'm so grateful to be getting sustenance I let it go.

'You assumed right. But you don't have to do all the ordering and paying. I'll do my bit.'

He winks, and smiles at the waitress as she brings our order. The croissant is warm and it's so delicious I could cry. I tear a piece off and offer it to him. He takes it with his mouth, licking a couple of my fingers as he does. He's either the sexiest man alive or the most calculating. Right now I couldn't give a damn. I'm too happy. When we finish up (it doesn't take long) we zip our coats back up and he leads me down the high street then turns me to the right. Suddenly I can see the sea ahead and an enormous, beautiful building. It has a black framework with lots of huge geometric pieces of coloured glass. I presume they're windows, but maybe some of them aren't, I can't tell from here. What I do know is, it's stunning. He points to it.

'Harpa. Concert hall, theatre, arts centre. A lot of opera and concerts happen there.'

'Fuck. It's beautiful.'

As we get closer I can see ships and boats in the harbour, which stretches out behind Harpa. I also see a little van with an open front right in front of us. The smell coming from it is something else. Einar grins at me.

'Sorry, I'm about to order for you again. You'll just have to accept it.'

He speaks to the older woman manning the cooking bit, in Icelandic. She laughs at something he says, looks at me curiously, who knows why, then throws food on the griddle, opens up two large bread rolls and spreads an orange sauce on them. Within minutes we are walking towards the road parallel to the sea, munching on these incredible sandwiches filled with fresh cooked lobster and a special 'secret' sauce. I've already had a croissant but it hardly touched the sides. This sandwich, however, is the absolute business. We walk along the pavement by the sea to the right of Harpa. The sea edge up to pavement level is piled with huge rocks of different sizes. There are signs you can stop and read, about whales and other sea animals to be found, and, sometimes, spotted in the bay. The air has a bite but I absolutely love how wild it feels here. I also love the metal Viking long ship sculpture that seems to be quite the tourist attraction, with couples and groups standing by it one after another to take photos. Opposite, far out to sea, is an incredible black mountain with white patches.

'What's that, Einar?'

'Mount Esja. She's a dormant volcano. No lava now but lots of snow in winter. Have to be careful of avalanches when you go and visit her. The next snow is definitely on the way so she'll be whiter soon.'

I love that she's a she. And she's calling me, I feel it. In my head I speak to her. *Hello, Esja, you are so beautiful.*

'*I've been waiting for you.*'

I don't hear it, I feel it. Esja has a living energy, old, so old, and I can tell she has stories to tell. I wrap my coat tighter around myself, slipping the sandwich wrapper into my pocket. Einar sees me shaking.

'Let's go and get a drink. You like White Russians?'

'Fuck yes.'

'Lebowski here we come!'

I don't know what Lebowski is but I'm happy to follow Einar and find out. Today is a good day. I look back towards Esja and breathe her in.

She's truly magnificent.

SO MANY RUSSIANS

Lebowski bar is amazing. I'm a bit tipsy, and I never want to leave it, ever, as long as I live. It has booths and music at the back, which is great fun, but we're at the front on a banquette. It's all trendy and cool with great music, and I can't believe they serve twenty-odd versions of a White Russian. They cost a mortgage each, as do the other cocktails, which I well know because I paid for the first round and my debit card burst into flames. But they're so yummy. Einar doesn't drink White Russians – they're too sweet, apparently – so he opted for Old Fashioneds, which are equally pricey. I started with a traditional White Russian, but then tried a Tropical Russian for my second, which is vodka, Tia Maria, cream and coconut syrup. It's truly delicious, and I fare well with sugary cocktails as they make me less wobbly and more warm and snuggly. We're on our third each now and my latest is a Pink Russian, which is strawberry flavoured and fantastic. Einar has gone a tiny bit cross-eyed, which suggests to me his cocktails are definitely full strength and not watered down like they would be in London, especially if tourists were being served.

He wraps his arm around my shoulders and I get a hit of that wonderful musk and clean hair smell that makes my heart sing. He puts his mouth against my ear.

'Thank you for coming to see me. It was brave.'

'Oh, I needed to get the hell away.'

'I like you, Tanz, but you have to know, I don't do relationships. I do wonderful affairs.'

My heart seizes for a second but then I refuse to compute what he's saying. I'm ablaze with lust and I don't believe for a fucking second he can't do relationships. I'll put money on the fact he's had a bad time and needs someone like me to make him feel safe. Look at us, having the best time ever. I'll show him and he won't be able to resist me. A wonderful affair can last twenty years with the right woman. I am that woman.

'You need to kiss me, Einar.'

He doesn't argue. He just looks at me and shakes his head.

'There's no stopping you, is there?'

'Or you. You don't have to only do affairs, Einar. You're probably just hurt. I can see it in those eyes. You have such beautiful eyes but there's pain there.'

'No, I'm through the worst of my hurt. I'm simply a libertine!'

'What, like the Marquis de Sade? You're a bit nicer than him. He wrote about torture and he ended up in an insane asylum.'

'I'm a nice libertine.'

'Yes. You are.'

God, I'm knackered and drunk. When we kiss, my head spins for more than one reason, but I'm not having this 'libertine' nonsense. He's met me now. I've flown to Reykjavík. He's not a child, he's older than me. I'll help him. I stop kissing him and lean on his shoulder.

'Where do you live by the way, Einar? You never said.'

'Not far from the harbour. With a flatmate who has a difficult girlfriend from Denmark. She's here this week and I can't be bothered with her or I'd invite you over. We don't want to be tiptoeing around her. No one at my summer house, though. All clear there and you're going to love it and get lots of work done. You want to go back to your room? You're nodding off.'

He's not wrong. Even in this state, I'm sad that he doesn't want me to come back to his place, but I get it. If his living arrangements are awkward, then I have to accept it. And I really need to sleep. I've been awake for about eight weeks, or that's how it feels. Lebowski bar is so close to my room it only takes five minutes until we're on my sofa, and Einar, the crazy bastard, is opening the bottle of red wine I bought. I ask for a can of Diet Coke that I left in the fridge and sip it, as he downs a glass of red. We clamber onto the bed side by side and sit up against the pillows. He plays music he thinks I'd like on his phone and I try to listen intently, but within minutes I fall into the deepest of exhausted sleeps.

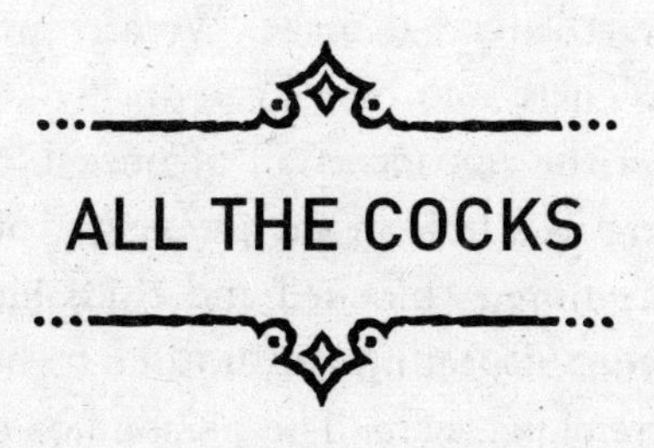

ALL THE COCKS

I am flying over Mount Esja, astride a giant sea eagle. I know what they look like because I watched a nature programme about them and they're bloody beautiful creatures. I see the shadow of its wingspan over the volcanic rock as I soar through the air. This is twice the size of any real eagle, but I'm not thinking about that as I ride the thermals. No, I'm breathing in the fresh, nourishing air and observing the water below, which is dark navy and dangerous-looking. Esja pounds with hot life, I can feel it. She is pulsing with magma and female intuition and controlled wrath. It's like I'm flying over myself on this giant brown-and-white-tailed bird. I've never felt so empowered or happy. I know as I fly that I have no worries, no job, no bills to pay. I am just a being, linked to the rock below, soaring through the skies, pounding and pulsing with the same lava, the same passion as the mother mountain. I lean into soft feathers as I steer my eagle to the left and glide in an arc. The eagle cocks its head to look at me. A pale green eye I've seen before. The fun, the pain, the hidden truths . . . And then the eagle begins to plummet towards the sea. It's seen something it wants beneath those waves and I will be collateral damage. We are speeding to my watery death. There's nothing I can do.

I don't feel the impact as all at once I'm now in the dark. I'm lying in a hole in the freezing ground. My face is covered, my nose is blocked and clods hit me all over. I can't breathe. Suffocating and no one to help me, but I know I will remain aware. The person covering me with wet earth is someone I love and I can't cry out, because I'm dead and trapped and will lie here for eternity, awake but not breathing.

I wake up sobbing and have no fucking clue where I am as it's so dark. A moment of orientation, and I comprehend that I'm in my hotel room, still fully clothed, back against pillows. I pat around and discover my phone is by my right hand on the bed. I squint into its illuminated screen and see it's 8 a.m. I've been lying like this for eight hours solid. I am dying for a pee, and I'm alone. Einar is not in the bed, and I also know with certainty that he's not anywhere in the room either. It's completely silent and empty. He's gone.

It takes me a few seconds more to remember that dawn won't be for another two hours here. I switch on the little lamp by my side of the bed. There's a glass of water that's been left there for me, which is quite sweet. I drink a few mouthfuls. The red wine bottle is empty on 'his' side and the glass stands in a small circle of spilled wine. I hope it hasn't bloody stained the wood. There's a piece of lined paper where Einar should be sleeping, pulled from my newly minted notebook, the one in which I hope to write the beginning of a masterpiece. On it I see, in a beautifully constructed cursive hand . . .

Sorry, I can never sleep until the early hours so I thought I'd leave, rather than wake you by bumbling about. See you tomorrow, darling x

No matter how much I try to see the good side of this, I can't help feeling he abandoned me when he wasn't having enough fun. Why is it so hard to lie next to someone who has flown all this way to see you? I'm well aware that I myself have never really liked sleeping next to anyone all night so this is a little hypocritical. But we have a bond, he and I, and we're only just getting to know one another. Would it have killed him to try to sleep?

I get up and go to the bathroom and refresh my glass from the tap. The water is cold as ice and delicious. I gaze out of my balcony window and see people wandering about, probably mostly on their way to work. The lights in the windows on the street are pretty. Feeling restless and rather alone, I decide to make the best of the fact I don't have too much of a hangover, I'm very awake and I probably have a few hours to kill if that Icelandic swine stayed up all hours. First, I have an eggy, hot shower, wash my hair and clean my teeth. Once I'm all dry and the hair is sorted I pull out a different, even warmer jumper than yesterday's and wear it over a T-shirt and my thick jeans. With a slick of Chapstick and a beanie to carry in my pocket, in case my ears can't take the cold, I don my parka and sparkly trainers and make my way out onto Laugavegur.

The hat immediately goes on; it feels like snow weather, it's so chilly. The coffee shop from yesterday is open so I pop in, and savouring the unmistakable scent of fresh baked goods, I order a takeaway coffee and get a warm croissant in a paper bag. I wander up and down the main broadway, nibbling the delicious pastry and sipping away, and despite my irritation at Einar, enjoy the festive feel of the lights in the windows, and absolutely love that there is an actual all-year-round Christmas shop that sells beautiful decorations. The other way up the road, I pass a place called Dillon Whiskey Bar. Einar mentioned this on our 'date' in London. Said it had some great live acts on and the best burgers in Reykjavík, plus many, many whiskies to choose from. I detest whisky but the live music bit sounded cool. As I step off the straight path and wander a little further, I stop dead when I see the most extraordinary thing. The picture is unmistakable on the window and I look twice before absolutely acknowledging that I am at the door of a penis museum. (Or Phallological Museum, to give it its proper title.) What the actual fuck is going on? I have to go in there. It says opening hours are 10 a.m. 'til 7 p.m. It's 9.39 a.m. now; I can wait another twenty minutes or so. I sit on a bench and text Einar.

I'm up and out. I have discovered the penis museum. Checkout of my place is 11 a.m. Reply by then, please, as I'll be floating about like a right lemon.

His reply is pretty instantaneous to be fair.

Sorry, lovely, went home and sat up with my flatmate. He and his girl just split up. I'm glad, but you have to show some sympathy, don't you? Glad you found our crazy little museum of willies. Will come and meet you outside your hotel at 11.15 a.m.

And with that one text he's utterly forgiven. With a big grin on my face I put away my phone and prepare to meet a load of chopped-off cocks.

'*Trust you to find the cocks.*'

'Frank. Trust you to show up now.'

'*I can't believe that douchebag left you to sleep on your own last night.*'

'He's on his way back. He just wasn't tired.'

'*Well, I didn't abandon you. Do you know you snore like an old sow when you're drunk?*'

'What the FUCK? Shut up!'

I can hear Frank's laugh.

'*At least he's letting you stay in his summer place. The prices here are mad. You'd be living on bread and jam for a year if you had to pay to stay here the rest of the week.*'

'See, he has his uses.'

'*One. He has that one use.*'

'You are soooooo jealous.'

'*And you fancy idiots. Enjoy the dicks.*'

'Why is everything you're saying so filthy?'

'*It's your dirty ears.*'

Just then the museum door opens. It's show time!

ENCHANTMENT

We're in the Icelandic supermarket, which isn't that different to a London one, just even more expensive. Einar looks like someone hit him in the face with a monkey-boot. His eyes are bleary, his skin is slightly mottled, with a few creases still not ironed out from his pillow, and he stinks of booze. I have no fucking idea if he should even be driving. He piles the basket with bottles of wine, bread, cheese and meat. He then picks up a packet of cakes. Little pink-topped ones.

'I think you'll like these.'

His voice is heavy with tiredness. He puts another pack in. That's twelve cakes. I hope he plans on eating most of them.

'Bloody hell, Einar, were you up the whole night?'

'I got two hours' sleep. Not unusual for me.'

'*Two hours?* Why did you stay up so long?'

He looks the teensiest bit uncomfortable at being grilled.

'Just talking to my friend, with wine. He was in a bit of a state. His woman had packed up and gone to a hotel.

This isn't unusual, their relationship is ridiculous. She expects too much, always. But that's what they're like. Tempestuous.'

'Well, you'd better grab yourself a nap when we get to the summer house.'

He puts the basket down ready to unload all the goodies onto the conveyor.

'I'm afraid that'll have to wait. I have work to do this afternoon. I will drop you there, get you settled, then drive to my meeting. Back for dinner later tonight. Sorry.'

I feel a stone settle in my belly. He asked me to come here, but now I'm afraid that I'm putting him out. I know he's stressed, he looked at his phone like it was a venomous snake when a message came through in the car, but I wouldn't dare ask him why. He's elusive enough without me pressuring him.

'That's okay. I said I wanted some peace, to write. As long as I get to snuggle up with you later.'

He smiles at me but he really does look fucked. What a life he leads. Who can work after two hours' sleep?

I put the bags into the boot of his car. It's a solid enough Skoda Octavia in dark blue. He's so flash, a Skoda seems a strange car choice for him, but I guess they buy the most reliable cars for weather changes over here. And everything's imported so I reckon cars must cost a bomb. I shiver as I get in the passenger seat and watch a few snowflakes fall. Wow, if it snows, it's going to look even more Christmassy here.

'Snow isn't forecast to get heavy until next week, Tanz, so don't worry, you won't get snowed in. Just a little flurry.'

I don't like people telling me what 'won't' happen. I'm not your average person. If it's going to happen against the odds, bet your bottom dollar it'll happen to me. But this snow is very light and already seems to be dissipating so I'm willing to believe, just this once.

As we drive, leaving the sea, the bay and Mount Esja behind us, I get a jump in my tummy. Off to a house in a foreign countryside with a relative stranger. Who the hell am I? I laugh to myself and Einar notices and twinkles.

'Enjoying yourself?'

'Just thinking how crazy everything is. Oh my giddy aunt, what's that? Is that a . . . ?'

'Glacier. Yes.'

'Holy shit, I've never seen a glacier in real life before. It's so beautiful.'

We are driving through stunning countryside. It's green and rocky and to the left is the bloody great bright-white glacier, while to the right is green land with dark mountains in the distance, and very widely spaced cabin-like houses. Plus, there are horses! Gorgeous sturdy ones with lots of fluffy hair and long manes.

'Oh wow, Einar! The horses!'

'Yes, they're very special. You can pay to ride one at the farm over there; they're extremely strong. We only have Icelandic horses here, no others. People outside Iceland want to own them and they can but once a horse leaves here it can never come back. We have such a low prevalence of disease here, once they're gone they stay gone. We don't even let equine *equipment* into the country unless it's brand new or completely disinfected.'

'Wow. I love how everything is kept pure. This place is like another planet. You have volcanoes next to glaciers, glaciers next to farmland, farmland next to . . . Jesus, STEAM . . . ?'

Einar throws his head back and laughs.

'Hot springs. They're everywhere. No ropes or warnings, you just know that if you put your hand in there, you'll cook it. They're not all boiling hot but many are. Next time you're in town, go to the outdoor swimming pool. It's like swimming in a warm bath. Naturally heated water from underground. We also have the Blue Lagoon, as well as other less touristy hot spas, where you can float and cleanse and have a beer if you want to, while the droplets freeze on your hair. You need to do a spa.'

'Wow. If I can't fit it in before I fly back, I'll need to come back another time. See the sights.'

He winks. I don't know what he's actually thinking. I'm hoping he likes me as much as I like him and this is him encouraging me to come and stay again, but it's so bloody hard to tell. I know one thing, though: I could never stay up all night on a regular basis like he does. I'd die. And here he is, driving the car and laughing and functioning and everything.

He puts on some ambient music and I nod my head to it as I take in the sights. We're now passing mountains, and the rocky landscape, shaped by magma eons ago, makes my heart sing. Also, to my delight, there are more and more trees. They're mostly birches. I know more about trees than I should. I love them. These look hardy and scrubby and like Christmas trees. I want to go and hug them.

They're skinnier than the oaks I hug at home but it's just all so exhilarating and new. Plus, I can't function without trees so it's nice to see there are actually plenty of them.

'What did you mean when you said you harnessed magic?'

He looks at me blankly. I can't believe he's forgotten our conversation.

'You said back in London that there's a lot of magic in Iceland and you harness it to live life to its fullest?'

'Oh, yes. Well, there are many powers you can harness to make your life more interesting. People always want to talk to me and are naturally attracted to my aura, because I'm open. I'm open to the magic.'

'Yes, but is that magic or "enchantment"? Enchantment isn't necessarily good magic. Isn't it selfish magic, to fool people into giving you what you want, or desire? I thought enchantment was leading people where you want them to go, like the Pied Piper.'

'Hahahaa. I don't think there's any difference. As long as you're not making a person do anything against their own will, then it's magical.'

'I don't even know that much about magic. I just know that I want to use whatever "magic" I have to help others. Doing stuff just to get what I want . . . well, I'm not sure that would end well. I always want the wrong things.'

I have no idea why I'm even saying this stuff. He brings out such a different side to me. He glances sideways at me and shrugs.

'I was open to you and you came towards me. Does that mean I enchanted you?'

I stick my tongue out at him.

'Maybe *I* enchanted *you.*'

He puts his hand on my leg as he drives. 'Maybe you did, you northern witch.'

BLOOD-RED ROWAN TREE

I cannot believe the place he's pulled up at. It's the most amazing, straight-out-of-a-posh-holiday-brochure cabin. There's a stoop outside to the right, with large rocking chairs on it with purple embroidered seat pads on them, like in a storybook. There's also a ledge that sticks out from the roof, high and sloped, so the chairs are sheltered. There are two floors and lots of massive windows. I'm in love within thirty-seven seconds of getting out of the Skoda. I spot a rowan tree, blooms almost blood red. There's a fucking rowan tree by the stoop; a magical tree by a magical cabin in a magical place. Everything else nearby is mossy or a bush. I love all of it. The birds out here in the extremely nippy air sound completely different to British birds. More otherworldly and piping, though I may just be romanticizing things a tad. Einar gets out of the driver's side and I run to him and wrap my arms around him. He lifts me up and I kiss him.

'This is so fucking gorgeous. I've never seen anywhere like this. Not in real life!'

He puts me down and starts taking shopping bags out of the boot.

'Wait until you see inside.'

We take the bags to the front door and he lets us in. When I walk through I have to stop and breathe, I'm so enraptured. High ceilings, huge windows, all wooden and natural-smelling. The kitchen and living room are completely open plan. Giant sofa and huge armchairs. Light streams in from every angle. I can see the open door to a bathroom, plus there's an open wooden staircase that I imagine leads to a bedroom or two. There are large, natural-coloured candles in clear glass, wooden shelves with books and vinyl records, plus a huge CD rack, filled to the top. The wine rack already holds a lot of bottles. Einar puts all the cold produce in the fridge, along with an extra three bottles of white, and places three bottles of red on the kitchen counter. The fridge looks full anyway, but he fills it more. He puts on an Ella Fitzgerald CD and rocks on his feet. He sinks down on the sofa, glancing at his phone again.

'I need to go soon.'

I walk to a silver-framed cafetière in the kitchen and pick up the new bag of coffee by it.

'You look so tired. Let me make you a coffee first.'

He doesn't argue and I fill the kettle and put it on. As it begins to boil, I sit by this crazy man and wrap my arms around him. Bury my face next to his ear. Smell his neck. He sighs and rubs a hand over his face. I brush against his lips and he responds with the tiniest of butterfly kisses, then I go and prepare him a coffee, good and black. He receives it gratefully and I sit next to him, leg against his, and sip my own. He gazes at me, such an unreadable look on his face.

'You're a good woman. Kind. Is this a nice place to spend time and write?'

'Of course it is. It's absolutely gorgeous.'

'Well, there's a full fridge, a load of wine and wood for the wood burner, which looks great but is especially helpful if the power goes out.'

'If the *what*?'

'Oh, don't worry, just in case there's a power cut. It doesn't happen often.'

'And you'll be here at night anyway, *right*?'

'Of course. And just know, the crime rate here is virtually zero. You are completely safe. If there was anywhere safe to be alone and with your own thoughts, it's here.'

'Thank you, Einar. I could never have afforded to come and do this, these cabins cost a bloody bomb, and it's like heaven.'

He smiles again at me, though I can't help seeing a cloud at the back of those green eyes. Who knows what's going on in there. Or maybe he's just hungover. He leans forward and gives me the most perfect soft kiss with his delicious cupid's bow lips, then stands.

'I must go. Treat everything like it's your own. My cousin sometimes uses the place so don't be disturbed by stuff in the drawers, they're just his and his wife's clothes. There are plenty of blankets and shawls too if you want to sit outside.'

A heavy weight settles in the pit of my stomach as he

gets back in the car. What the hell is wrong with me? I've trained myself to never be needy with men. I don't want to be 'that' woman. But there's something about the way he holds himself back and does as he pleases and disappears at will that makes him like a drug to me. I don't want him to go, I want him to find it impossible to leave me. But leave he does, beeping his horn as he spins his wheels like a boy racer.

And now I'm completely alone, like I could never be in the built-up maze that is London. Hugging my arms around myself, I watch as the snow returns, right on cue, this time much fatter flakes landing on the earth before me and not melting. My mouth opens wide as I look up and realize there's a bird circling overhead. I wonder if I'm mistaken but I know I'm not. It's an eagle. It's a fucking *eagle*. Just like I dreamed, but I'm not riding this one. Einar was right, this place is rammed with magic.

I decide I should utilize the rest of today's light and sit on a purple-cushioned rocking chair outside. Despite saying I'm here to write, I also have a couple of light novels with me, nothing too testing, and reading transports me from all thought, which is exactly what I want right now. I want to take in the bird noises and breathe the fresh air and drink another hot coffee with some easy words in front of me. Dostoevsky be damned. I go inside and grab a pile of wool blankets from the sofa that I think are placed there exactly for this reason. I make another coffee, take a packet of those pink cakes, just in case I fancy one, and wrapping myself in loads of layers of warm wool, I sit down and gently rock. The coffee tastes fab in the fresh air and when

I nibble one of the cakes I'm pretty close to ecstasy. It's almondy, almost like a Bakewell tart in flavour, and there's no way I'm stopping at one. I cannot believe how much rubbish I'm putting in my face today, but I'm on holiday. That's what I'll keep telling myself until the guilt fucks off again. The eagle has gone now, but the other cries of smaller birds are lonesome and musical at the same time. I wonder if birds ever get lonely. I try not to get lonely even though I'm single and live alone, but then I always have somewhere to go to or something to do to avoid my own thoughts. Plus, I have Inka, my silky black cat, who's another beating heart in my home. Maybe to really process life, I needed to be completely cut off and that's why the universe has brought me here. I actually believe that loneliness is simply FOMO: you think other people are doing something more exciting than you are so you feel abandoned and left out. I've had more than my share of 'excitement' since I met Sheila at Mystery Pot. Ghosts and shocks and unexpected adventures, as well as more danger than I ever wanted or expected in my whole life. So I resolve to savour every moment at this cabin and not even entertain the thought of loneliness. Maybe I'll finally learn how to meditate properly.

I bloody doubt it but it's worth a try.

THE WEIRDNESS

So I get a whole hour of peace, snow, reading, eating pink cakes (four, I've eaten *four*! What's wrong with me?) and blowing hot breath on my frozen hands before something weird happens. Something weird always happens to me, so it's no fucking surprise when I think I see the shadow of a person out of the corner of my eye, beside the rowan tree. Disconcerted, my head whips round, but then when I focus on the place I saw them, there's no one there. I tell myself it may have been the shadow of a bird flying over. The light is dimming now so they'll all be headed wherever they go to roost at night, surely?

It freaks me out enough to send me inside, though. I close the doors and go to the record player on the far side of the living room and, glancing at the pile of vinyls, I see an Abba album. This makes me laugh. It must belong to Einar's cousin, as I can't imagine Einar listening to Abba. I put it on. I'm pretty sure it's a clinical fact that you can't sing along to Abba and be scared at the same time. I glance furtively towards the rowan tree. Definitely no one there.

I then locate one of those clicky oven igniter things in a drawer in the kitchen, and use it to light a bunch of candles. With lamps, candles, the heating warming the radiators (I reckon it's on a timer) and Abba, who wouldn't be chirpy? I open a bottle of heavy red wine, which seems fitting for a day like today, and settle into the comfy sofa with my book, ear cocked for an incoming text from Einar. That's when I hear the voice. Not Frank, the centre of my soul, my inner compass.

'He's not coming back. Look outside.'

The snowfall's now back with a vengeance; it's getting thicker and it's settling. There's at least an inch of it on the ground. But Einar said it wouldn't get that bad. Anyway, surely they're used to driving in snow over here? Of course he's coming. I don't want to message him and bug him, but that flippin' voice has worried me slightly, so I do.

Hello, you. It's still snowing, will you be okay to come back?

He doesn't reply and I watch as darkness falls outside and the view of the mountains and scenery winks out into almost thorough blackness. I carry on with side two of Abba, plus more wine, and read another chapter of my book. My phone pings.

Hello, darling. I'm so sorry, one of my snow tyres is flat. Won't be able to fix it until tomorrow as I'm working later than expected. Also, I'm in first thing so better anyway if I stay in town tonight in case it

gets worse. I'm very sorry to do this. I promise you're safe, and I bought plenty of provisions. Wood burner is set up and ready to go, plus a huge wood pile outside. The instructions by the side are in English as well as Icelandic. Stay warm and comfy and enjoy. See you tomorrow.

Holy crap, not only am I now completely abandoned for the night, but he didn't even call me, he waited for me to ask then sent a fucking text. I take three long, deep breaths and attempt to talk some sense into myself. I did not come to Iceland as his girlfriend, he invited me to come over and do some writing at this place. He also didn't promise he would spend every night with me. I wanted him to but that's not the same. Apart from anything else, he has a job, he's working and this place is an hour in the snow from town. He'll get his tyre fixed and come and see me soon enough. Also, if he's at work, he probably can't call me. I need to get a grip or I'll scare him off. He's been generous and lovely and this place is stuffed with food and drink. The wood burner will make it even nicer. Time to pull up my big girl pants and actually embrace being on my own in a beautiful land. That's what I wanted, right? *Right?*

Okay, so I cry for five minutes. Just to let out the disappointment. I mean, my life is rather an emotional cocktail shaker at the moment, rattling me hither and thither. After everything else that's gone on lately, I certainly wasn't supposed to fall for a raggy-haired crazy man who doesn't sleep. Not that I'm in love, obviously. I'm just a bit besotted. My phone pings again as I'm blowing my nose. I grab it but my heart sinks when I see it's from Neil, asking how I am. I'm not bloody answering that.

Right, *enough*, plan time. There's a whole chicken in the fridge. I'm going to put that in the oven, light the wood burner and drink as much wine as I want. I will bury myself in cosiness. Maybe even watch a film from the DVD collection.

Fuck all this drama.

I'm on holiday.

SQUEAL LIKE A PIG

'So you're on your fucking own out there?' Milo is completely scandalized.

'Well, he did offer me use of his place to write in and he didn't technically say we'd be here together. But I hoped he'd be here at night.'

'What a dick.'

'He's not a dick, his tyre's buggered, he's at work first thing and it's snowing like a bastard.'

'Well, I don't like the sound of you marooned in a cabin. This isn't like one of those cute Christmas films with a sexy lumberjack. It's more like fucking *Deliverance* with snow. That Einar's definitely going to be squealing like a pig when I get my hands on him.'

'Stop it. I rang because I'm a bit scared of going to sleep on my own, don't make it worse.'

'Have you locked the doors?'

'Of course.'

'So just leave a light on and play some music or something. And as soon as you can, get back to Santa's village and book a flight home.'

'Who knows if I can get back if the snow gets worse tomorrow. Plus, I can't just fly back straight away, there's things I'd like to do.'

'Eurgh, you can't still like him? He didn't even stay with you in the hotel. There's something wrong there.'

'I just think he has a full life.'

'Okay.'

I've called him because despite the warmth, the candles, the cooked chicken and the wine, I've started feeling a bit uncomfortable. Like I'm not on my own here. I didn't feel it earlier when I arrived, but fifteen minutes ago, just as it hit 9.30 p.m., the hairs on the back of my neck began to stick up. I was aware it could just be fear still from seeing that shadow, but that was ages ago and I was actually comfy and nodding off when suddenly I sat bolt upright and my skin started crawling. In my almost-asleep state I could have sworn I heard someone sobbing. I didn't have the TV on, the music had stopped and I was happily listening to the gentle crackle of the wood burner. I'd actually nearly finished my book, a light romance that needed very little concentration. But after that strange weeping, I tried to call Einar and it went straight to voicemail. The sting of him not answering had to be assuaged immediately before I started overthinking, so I decided to call my best mate from my home town, Milo, who would never ignore my call. (And I'm now convinced I dreamed the crying noise.)

We chat for half an hour while I watch the wood begin

to burn down. I realize I'm going to have to go to the wood pile at about the same time my phone makes that 'low charge' sound.

'Oh shit, Milo. I need to plug my phone into the charger. I also need to get more wood from the pile on the stoop.'

'GO OUTSIDE?'

'Will you stop it?! I'll keep you on loudspeaker while I nip out and grab a bunch of logs.'

I take the phone to the door and undo the latch. It's absolutely Baltic out there. I don't want to go out but actually once I'm grabbing the wood, the sound of snow falling is soft and soporific. It's when I'm closing the door behind me again that all the lamps go out. I scream like a motherfucker and I hear Milo shouting at his end, obviously freaked out.

'Sorry, Milo, sorry, I think there's been a power cut. I'm trying the light switch now and it's not working. And the clock on the oven's gone off. I'm going to have to put the phone down while there's still a bit of power left in it.'

'Bloody hell, Tanz, are you okay? I was joking about *Deliverance*. Do you have enough candles?'

'Yup. Loads of them, plus about a year's worth of wood for the burner. I can sleep on the sofa by the fire if needs be.' I let out a shaky breath. I'm so scared but I'm not telling him that.

'I'm sorry, Tanz. Call me back as soon as you have power. I'm now shitting my pants and I'm not even there.'

'It's okay, I'm a big girl, it'll be fine. Love you, pet.'

'Love you!'

And here I am, shedding lonely tears in the dark, wondering why my life always goes wonky.

FRANTIC COUPLING

It takes me a little while to gather myself, then I put more wood in the burner and light the huge six-wick bad boy in a glass holder on the large dining table, which dominates the open-plan living room/kitchen. The light from the candle is pretty bloody impressive and it smells of beeswax, which is lovely. I pour another glass of red for fortification and wonder what to do. My phone's not got enough charge for phone calls; I have no idea how long there'll be a power cut and I don't want to lose that tiny link with the outside world. The snow is falling heavily outside and with just candles lit and no electric light it's easier to see out there, as it's not as dark as it seemed. I stand at the window and search for signs of life. It looks quite beautiful, like everything's coated in icing sugar. I text Einar to let him know there's a power cut. I keep it short. I'm getting sick of him not replying now. I'm not hearing anything from Frank in my head either. If he's supposed to be my guardian angel, he's got very little to say for himself tonight. Saying that, I have this gut feeling, one that I'm not that happy about. Something's pulling me upstairs. I popped my head up there earlier, and saw a sprawling bedroom with an en suite and a smaller one without one. Big beds, lots of wood, lovely old-school bedspreads. But it'll be all dark and shadowy up there now, so why on earth would I want to go and scare myself any more?

I sit on the settee and let the warmth from the fire calm me. The fact I'm being urged to go upstairs doesn't mean I have to go right now, does it? After a while of fear-induced inertia, I spot a metal and glass lantern with a chonky cream pillar-candle in it by the front door. I light the candle, close the little glass panel on the front and, cradling my wine in the other hand for comfort, I go upstairs, slowly. Halfway up, a step creaks and I nearly jump out of my skin. One of the less fun things about everything being wooden here is that there's plenty of creaking.

At the top of the stairs, I pause, then go into the bigger bedroom and gasp. The white of the snow outside is eerily bright through the oversized windows. It looks beautiful. This big room is well illuminated and, more importantly, there's a 'feeling' in here. It's hugely protected. This room would take up a sword and cut someone's throat for you. It's incredible. Plus, having only peeked in briefly earlier, I hadn't taken in the nest of hurricane lamps on a table at the foot of the bed, or the fact there's also a wood burner in here. When the lamps are all lit, and the wood burner is catching, which doesn't take very long because it was already set up inside with kindling and chopped logs, I suddenly feel much better. It's chilly but I know the burner and the heavy blankets will sort that. I decide I'm going to stay up here after all. The room makes me feel safe, like my healing angel Jemima does when she shoots warm light through me. But there's something extra and undefinable to the feeling. A dark edge that matches well with my own. Not threatening, just firm and taking no shit. If there's a 'taking-no-shit' spirit about, making the room safer, then I'm totally here for it.

I skip back downstairs and get my little case, which I unpack in the bedroom, now dancing with light from the flames of the wood burner. I check my phone again, which still has no reply from Einar and is now on eight per cent battery power, because I accidentally had my Bluetooth switched on and it ate most of what was left, *dammit*. I go back down again and extinguish the massive candle on the table; no point wasting wax if this power cut is going to last more than a few hours. I then put the cooked chicken, some tomatoes and brie on a plate with a hunk of bread and cover it with tin foil to take upstairs with me in case I get hungry later, and grab the rest of the bottle of red. No point being without provisions. I decide I've now done enough trips up and down the stairs to equal a short stint on a running machine, and that makes me feel a bit better about the numerous cakes I stuffed down my neck earlier. I also know there's another daft novel in my case if I want to read by candlelight. This all feels much more like a glamping trip than it did forty-five minutes ago when I was scared bloody witless. I'm not scared of being on my own usually, but there's a difference between being on my own with neighbours listening through the walls and this kind of 'on my own', which really is isolated and cut off.

I get under the heavy covers on the bed, propping myself up against a bunch of thick cushions, and watch the snow fall past the window. I'm still on high alert, but not terrified any more. The feeling in this room is extraordinary. Plus, I've brought up a giant knife from the kitchen, so no matter what happens, I won't be going down without a fight. It's while I'm like this, no TV, no music, no distractions, that my thoughts bounce back to the penis museum from earlier. Of course they do. That mad place where I got a bit queasy at the sight of the sperm whale's giant willy and the squashed-up little mess in a jar which was a real human penis. The man had donated it, obviously proud of his member, and the amputation and pickling process didn't seem to have gone to plan. If I'm honest, I liked the 'made-up' penises better, the ones attributed to creatures from Icelandic folklore. Trolls and all that. It's because of the museum that I came across the Yule Lads. There was a description of these thirteen 'lads' that cause mischief at Christmas. They appear on different nights for thirteen days leading up to the big day and do really weird things, and perhaps leave a gift or not, depending on how naughty you've been. I can't remember all of their names but I know that one is a spoon licker and another appears to eat people's yoghurt, and then there's the one that slams doors to keep everyone awake. I love the fact they're called 'lads', like they are in the north of England, but also that they were far darker further back in history, even though they're now just cheeky pranksters. It all sounded a bit nuts and funny this morning, but since I've experienced the weather and the terrain first-hand, as winter draws in here, the 'Yule Lads' tale takes on that slightly gothic quality that would give a scary thrill to any child, Christmas or not. I can imagine them right now, outside in the snow causing all sorts of creepy mayhem – much worse stuff than licking spoons.

I check my phone. So little power left. It's knocking on midnight and I wonder if I should read but as I lie back, the rich red wine and the dancing of the firelight begin to take effect and my eyes start to close. I cannot believe I'm actually falling asleep.

I can't believe it even more when my eyes open inwardly on a very real-feeling vision, in broad daylight, where I'm creeping cautiously up to a stone barn in the sprawling Icelandic countryside. The brickwork looks dilapidated but it's not actually falling down, just needs some work. And it has a turf roof, which is something I've not seen in real life before. It's chilly but not freezing, the sun is shining and I'm wearing strange brown boots that definitely aren't mine. I think I can hear a goat somewhere, and the mossy, rocky ground morphs into lava-grey hills in the distance. It's starkly beautiful here. As I reach the door of the barn and quietly inch it open to look inside, it's not a goat I spy. There are two people there, entwined in the hay, locked in an embrace. I can only view them from the shoulders down, as I'd have to open the door fully to see them properly and I daren't do that, but the noises they're making are quite something, and they're absolutely naked. I can see a lot more of his body, as he's on top, and it's strong and muscular. He begins to move down her quivering torso as I watch, kissing his way around her belly, and lo and behold he has a fulsome dark-brown beard and matching thick head of hair – an Icelandic look, there's no mistaking it, though darker than a lot of the blokes I saw in town earlier. I feel like I should turn away when his mouth comes to rest between her legs, but boy, seeing him in action and hearing her lose her shit like this is extremely erotic. I notice a feeling of jealousy inside me that belongs to 'someone else'. I sense a charge of heated fury that I have to keep bottled up. Whoever's eyes I'm looking through was wretched and desperate as they watched this frantically pleasureful coupling. When the woman in the hay seems to reach a pitch of near hysteria, he slides back up to kiss her face and they move together as one until they both climax noisily, the lucky sods. The person whose eyes I'm looking through emits a cry of pure despair as she watches them in their passionate clinch, and I can't help wondering who this is, spying on the lovers.

Before I can think of finding any clues, I hear a different kind of cry and suddenly I'm not watching the end of an intense sex show any more. I'm Tanz, in a strange bedroom in a far-flung land, waking up in a cold room where the wood burner has gone out, and there's no mistaking it, there really is the sound of crying coming from outside in the darkness. I look at my phone and it's on two per cent and it's 6.30 a.m. Quite a while 'til the sun comes up but at least it's not the middle of the night now, and whether I like it or not I have to go and see what's outside because I'm definitely not dreaming that noise. Someone is weeping out there in the freezing cold.

I wrap the top bed cover around me and creep to the

window. Thank fuck I have socks on, my toes would probably freeze and snap off otherwise. I look out over a pure white vista. The snow has stopped. There's no sound. I think of opening the double-glazed window to hear better, but then I see something. There's someone moving around, about twenty feet beyond the rowan tree. A shadow is what it looks like. The shadow of a person.

Fucksake.

BIG-COAT WEATHER

Einar's cousin has drawers full of quality stuff. I just found the biggest, fattest cable-knit jumper, along with several other sweaters in different styles. I've also found wellies and hiking boots in a cupboard downstairs by the front door. Men's and women's, lots of pairs. I know this place houses guests sometimes, but I'm still stoked that there's actually a pair of snow boots with thick grip, just waiting for me, only a tiny bit too big. The giant socks in another drawer take care of that. There are also some massive insulated jackets, so much warmer than the coat I brought. I wrap myself right up, ending in a jacket with a hood that stretches so far in front of me when it's done up at the neck, it looks like a tube with fur around the front. I'm about to head for the door, carrying a lantern with a great big lit candle and a wooden handle, when I get an idea. I rifle through the main three drawers in the kitchen and find what I suspected would be there at the back of the second one. A big battery-powered torch. BINGO! I can hardly move the top half of my body I'm so layered up, but I don't care. I hate being cold and it's early morning in fucking Iceland. The freeze here is serious.

As I open the stoop door, I'm struck by the twinkly loveliness of the snow on the rowan tree as the torchlight hits it, plus the sparkle on the rocks and bushes all around the place. The birds don't seem to be up yet, so there's no sound but a gentle breeze on the branches, and the snow muffles even that. The air is freezing but as fresh as any I've ever experienced. Frank is still noticeable by his absence, but as I step forwards, down the two stairs from the stoop and onto the snowy, crunchy ground, I hear a voice in my head. Quiet and infinitely calm.

'*Don't be afraid. She won't hurt you.*'

That's all I hear just before quiet sobbing kicks off in the bushes twenty feet away. Before I wasn't sure if it was a child crying or not, but now I can tell it's definitely a woman. Holy shit, I'm scared, but still I walk towards the sound. Partly because there's nowhere to run, and partly because I know I have to. I shine the torch in front of me, but can't see anything. The sound gets closer but there's nothing but snow and rocks and plants to see. Until I hear that voice again. Calm and warm, but very firm.

'*Switch off the torch.*'

Christ, my heart is already smashing in my chest. I'm out here alone and now I'm supposed to switch off my light source? Fuck me, I'm not even that bloody brave a person. Why me? Actually, I know why me. I'm the one that's here, that's why, and I've already heard that I'm not going to get hurt, so here goes nothing. I close my eyes for a second, take a breath and then switch off the torch. The crying is now about six feet in front of me, and as soon as the torch is off, I make out a shadow. The darkness solidifies somewhat and I 'feel' as well as see a woman with curly, long dark hair and a pretty face, around forty, sitting on the ground in the snow, staring straight at me and crying. She's lost someone, I can sense it, and she doesn't know how to find them again. She points behind her, towards the hills. There's a huge dark mark soaking her top. I can only imagine it's blood. She glares back at me, puts her hands together as if in prayer, then disappears, just like that. I look all around myself, like she might reappear, and I sink into the snow, overcome with her despair. She was so sad and lost and I could feel her pain, right in my chest. What the fuck happened to her? How am I supposed to handle shit like this all on my own?

I can't even stand up, I'm so weighed down by clothes. Instead, I sit here and start to snivel. To my shame, I'm not only crying for the poor woman I just saw whimpering on the ground. I'm crying for me, scared in the wilderness on my own, and for the fact that no matter how much I try to bury it, something's very 'off' with Einar, and once again I've been an absolute idiot for a bloke, this time for one that I hardly know. How I wish I wasn't such an arse. The tears flow as I consider how the hell I'll get back to civilization with no phone to call anyone and the roads blocked by snow. I'll just have to stay here, eating cold food and being haunted by a ghost lady. *How did I even get into this?* Like a Gateshead Humpty Dumpty, I manage to roll myself onto my knees in the snow, and that's when I see a light. I nearly poo my pants when a battery-operated lantern comes levitating around the side of the cabin. For a moment I scrabble round for a suitable rock or stick to use as a weapon, until I see the size and shape of the person carrying the lamp and then a toothy smile in a rosy face.

'Hellooooo.' A deep female Icelandic voice, which sounds like it's weathered a lot of cigarettes. I could bloody cry I'm so happy to see another woman. A real one, not a ghostly, shadowy one crying in the bushes. She reaches out her hand and helps me stand. She's wearing massive mitten thingies. She's so cute.

'Oh my God, where did you spring up from?'

The lamplight on her face shows an open, warm smile and wide-spaced round eyes.

'I live half a mile up the road. I saw your lights on just before the power went out. Tiny beams in the distance. Then they suddenly extinguished, so I waited to see if the cut would end, then thought I'd come and see if everything's okay. I have a back-up generator so I'm prepared for any power shortages.'

'Wow, you walked half a mile?'

'I love hiking. And I don't mind the snow.'

'You are now officially my favourite person ever. Come inside! I'm Tanz by the way.'

'Hello, Tanz, I'm Birta.'

She follows me in and I light the big bastard candle again on the table and begin to build up the wood burner. She takes over and is a total whizz at it. She builds it high enough up that it doesn't smoke into the room at all when first lit, it goes straight up the flue. Then she asks if I have bread. Next thing you know we're toasting slices on forks against the flames and eating them lathered in butter, with a glass each of a newly opened bottle of red.

'It's not technically morning yet, Tanz, so this is allowed.'

I laugh from deep inside, relief as much as anything. Birta, with her coat off, is wearing the most gorgeous jumper in all swirly colours, with blue jeans and sensible hiking shoes, and has long strawberry-blonde hair with what looks like silver streaks in it. I think she's a few years older than me, but she also looks like she's never worn make-up in her life and has great skin. One of those rosy-cheeked, wholesome faces that make you trust that everything's going to be fine. Right now I want to squeeze those cheeks, then bow down at her feet in gratitude. We grab a big blanket each when we've finished our toast and I curl up at the fire end of the sofa, while she sinks into the armchair on the other side, so we're both being warmed.

'So, Tanz, what are you doing here on your own?'

'Long story. I flew over from London after I met Einar, who owns this place, and he said I could use it as a writing retreat. I thought he'd be here too but he's busy, then the snow came . . .'

'Gagh, men. How long have you known him?'

I'm almost too ashamed to tell her.

'I met him twice.'

She laughs. It's a full-throttle lady growl.

'Oh my, you're worse than I am. I used to be a fool for love. Not any more. I live over there on my own, off grid and away from ridiculous men. They're not worth the hell they bring.'

'Oh no, did someone break your heart?'

'Of course. Doesn't everyone get their heart broken at one time or another?'

This sounds very poignant in her accent. Once again I'm astounded at how good everyone's English is here.

'So you live on your own in the middle of nowhere then?'

'Oh yes. It's beautiful here. And I'm a potter and a painter so it's perfect for me. I go to town for provisions when I need to. Car's not working right now, but I already stocked up for two months so I'm fine.'

'Woah, you're one of those creative people who live under the radar.'

'I am indeed. Can I ask you something, Tanz?'

'Yes, of course.'

'What were you doing sitting in the snow outside when I got here?'

I really like this woman's energy, so I don't want her to think I'm a maniac on our first meeting. I'll leave it until at least our third date.

'Oh, I thought I heard something, now I reckon it was a bird or an animal and I was just being jumpy. Then I fell over and felt a bit sorry for myself so I was having a cry.'

'Always good to cry it out.'

'It is. How long do you think the power will be off?'

'Hard to say, but it's usually quite quick. The snow wasn't forecast until next week so maybe there's just been a little blip locally.'

'Right. So I'm pretty much stuck here until the cavalry

arrives. But my phone is dead so I can't let the cavalry know I'm here.'

'Okay. Well, come to mine. I have a generator and some fun things to do for the day. I can give you a lesson in the stranger parts of Icelandic culture.'

'Even stranger than the penis museum?'

'The what?'

She looks mystified.

'The Phallological Museum, off Laugavegur. Lots of willies of animals and a man, plus plaster casts of cocks of real men and mythological ones.'

'I'm so sorry! Of course, that place. I've never visited.'

Thinking about it, I suppose it's like living in London and not visiting somewhere that has opened specifically for tourists. Also, not everyone is attracted by the thought of gazing on a room full of amputated members. My little mam would have an actual heart attack. Speaking of which, I've not phoned her for days. I ran off to Iceland and kept schtum before I left. She usually hears from me most days. I'm going to have a lot of explaining to do when my phone's back up and running.

'So, Tanz, come on, let's have some fun. I'm not always up for visitors but I like you.'

I laugh. She's a card this one. Without much thought I climb off the sofa and launch myself into her chair to give her a major bear hug. She hugs me back with all her might. She smells amazing and she's very warm.

'Do I need to bring anything?'

'A bottle of wine in case you don't like mine. Apart from that, we're all good. You can critique my ceramics.'

I climb back onto my perch, wrapping the blanket around me.

'Sounds like a euphemism.'

She cocks her head for a moment, then seemingly recalling what euphemism means, laughs her raspy laugh. She also pulls out some baccy and papers and begins to make a roll-up. So I wasn't wrong, she's a smoker. *Just call me Jessica Fletcher*. Part of me is worried that if I leave here, Einar may show up and find me gone, but deep down I know very well that he isn't going to show up. Anyway, I'll leave a note, and I don't intend to be away too long. It'll just be nice to have some company. And Birta has said she'll teach me some Icelandic cultural stuff, which will be a bonus and make me look less of an absolute chump when I fly back to England and face the wrath of my friends and mother.

'I hope you don't mind, I like to smoke as I walk. Would you like one?'

'Why not.'

Wine for breakfast, and the fact it's still dark as night when it's supposed to be morning by now, seems to have turned me into a different person. But fuck it, in for a penny, in for a pound. Maybe the universe hasn't totally lost its mind, because at least I've been sent a friend in my hour of need. One who smells of smoke and patchouli.

Definitely my kind of girl.

TREE FRIEND

The walk to Birta's is really quite lovely. The silence, the crunch of the snow, the breath-stealing landscape as the sky begins to lighten. And it feels very good to be exercising, stretching the legs. Though I'm not sure chuffing on a ciggie doesn't slightly erase some of the good of trudging half a mile in heavy snow boots. Birta points to a tree a few feet away from our path as we walk, and waves at it.

'I count that tea-leaved willow as a friend. They're usually more bush-sized but that one is a proper tree. She absolutely pushed against the boundaries and went to the edges of possibility. I'm proud of her.'

I try not to cough as I smoke the last of my skinny cigarette. I give a wave to the willow too, just to be polite.

'No offence, Birta, but are you a bit of a witch?'

'Depending on your perception of that word, I'm probably a lot of a witch.'

She's very easy to laugh with.

'Also, Tanz, did you notice the wonderful rowan tree outside your back door?'

'Of course. I was surprised to see it.'

'Rowans are one of the trees we get a lot of here, not as many as the birches and the poplars, but that particular one is a beauty. When I found you, my torch caught the clusters of red berries with snow on them and I nearly cried out. But we'd not spoken yet and I didn't want you to think I was mad. Though I am pretty mad.'

'Ditto.'

'I think from the positioning she was planted there deliberately. Which would make sense as it's the Tree of Life in Celtic mythology and symbolizes courage, wisdom and protection. They used to make crosses from the wood, bound with red thread, as a form of protection. And if you look at the bottom of rowan berries, there's a pentagram shape embedded in every one.'

'Holy shit, I thought I knew about trees but obviously I need to read more. That is so cool. I wonder who planted it?'

The sky is definitely getting lighter as we walk. Not bright light, not yet, just a shift in tone to a softer, misty grey.

'Rowan trees can live for two hundred years, so who knows how old it is or who planted it.'

'Two hundred years? Wow. I love that there's a pentagram on the berries. I'm going to have a look when I get back later.'

We're off the main track now for real. We pass through a pretty dense patch of birches, then walk uphill a little towards what I can now see is an old stone building with a leaky-looking roof. Before we get out of the copse, I spot something from the corner of my eye and stop. Birta also stops and regards me curiously.

'Are you all right, Tanz?'

'Erm . . . I'm not being funny, but did you just see someone?'

'Where?'

I look towards the tree where I just saw the dark shadow of 'someone'.

'It was a shadow of a person. They had long straight hair. Tall.'

She scrunches her face up, looking around.

'I can't see anyone.'

'Nor can I now. It was . . .'

'What?'

'I had this dream. Oh fuck, I don't know you well enough. You'll think I'm insane.'

'Come inside and tell me about it. You'll never be crazier than me.'

'Good to know.'

SEVENTIES CHIC

Nothing I say can truly describe how cool Birta's place is. Every damn thing is vintage. A lot of orange and brown. Big rugs, warm crocheted blankets over voluminous armchairs, plus a leaky roof with a red plastic bucket under the drips, and to top it off a massive fireplace. There are paintings and ceramics everywhere. Her ceramics are mostly blue and sensual in nature. Just looking at them, I want to cup them in my hands. The paintings are of rough seas and lonely trees. Full of feeling. She's incredibly talented. I don't, on the whole, fancy women. But if I did, I'd fancy this absolute powerhouse of passion, in her vintage clothes and no make-up. Birta is awesome. Truth be told, I am girl-crushing hard right now.

She makes sure the fire is lit in the living room within ten minutes. It shoots out a lot of heat and smells incredible. She lights incense next, then leads me to the kitchen. This whole place is a treasure trove. It actually costs more money than people understand to get original vintage stuff like this and I suspect some of it might be reproduction but it looks fantastic. Her coffee maker is cream and brown and the glass jug that the coffee goes into has flowers painted on it. She puts it on and goes to her clunky, square yellow fridge. Comes back with big fat scones.

'I made these. Delicious with my homemade bilberry jam.'

She puts four in a drawer in a huge Aga-like oven. It's warm in here so that must always stay on. There's also a buzzing noise coming from a little side room off the kitchen, which I assume is the back-up generator.

'Oh my goodness, woman, I'm not supposed to eat those. I'm an actress and am supposed to live off sawdust, lettuce and despair.'

'I thought you said you came here to write?'

'I came here hoping to write my first thing. I actually pretend to be other people for money.'

'How exciting. Most people would happily be someone else for free.'

'So true. You know, Birta, you're like a fictional character. People spend their lives dreaming about living like this. You're actually doing it. And your place is gorgeous, like a 1970s exhibition.'

She smiles then puts the warmed scones on a plate on the kitchen table, next to a butter dish, and places down a jar of what must be her bilberry jam, already open with a tiny spoon in it.

'Here, sit . . .'

She pulls out a wooden seat for me, then places a steaming mug of coffee in front of me. The mug is orange, and made of thick clay with some kind of opaque white glaze.

It feels substantial when I pick it up. I just know she made it. She sits opposite me and we butter our scones.

'Right, we have food and coffee, Mrs Actress Person. Now you can tell me about your dream.'

'Really? You'll think I'm crazy.'

'Then we can be crazy together.'

'Okay, so the other night I dreamed of a man with a beard standing looking over a cliff edge into the sea. Since I arrived here I've already worked out that men with beards are not thin on the ground and I'm pretty sure the dream was in Iceland, I could tell by the landscape. It was dark and he was very still. I got scared that he was going to jump. But then I saw this shadow of a person emerge from a bit further off. I couldn't tell if they were male or female, but I'm now pretty positive that he was male. He was watching the beardy suicide-man, but then he turned towards me and I could suddenly see his eyes, only they weren't so much eyes as portholes to another dimension. It was like they were made of starlight. I didn't try to speak to him or anything as I was so shocked, I ran off. In fact, I woke up with such a jump I terrified my cat. I still have the scabs on my leg to prove it.'

Birta laughs. 'My two cats are asleep in the bedroom. You should meet them later.'

'Awesome. We witchy women have to have at least one cat!'

She raises her mug in agreement.

'Anyway, when we were coming through the trees earlier I could have sworn I saw exactly the same shadow person. I even thought I caught a glimpse of someone by the rowan tree last night. I've had a lot of freaky shit happen to me recently. But shadow people?'

Birta nods and bites her scone. These scones are so incredibly delicious. I'm going to need to hit the gym like nobody's business when I get back to reality, but right now I'm savouring the comfort of carbs, coffee and excellent company. She doesn't look perturbed by my story at all; she looks more thoughtful than anything else. Suddenly she jumps up and goes to the bookshelf in an alcove next to the Aga thingy. There are more shelves stuffed with books in the living room. This lass is definitely a reader. She runs her finger along the tatty and not-so-tatty spines of her books until she finally finds what she's looking for and pulls out a fairly slim tome and sits again.

'Have you heard of the *Huldufólk*?'

A little gong goes 'bong' in my head but I'm not sure why.

'No, what's that?'

'The *Huldufólk* are the Hidden Ones. The "Hidden Folk".' She fingers through the pages as she speaks. 'They're also sometimes referred to as elves and people love telling stories about Icelanders believing in elves, teasing us. But elves aren't tiny little fairies in strange fancy dress. They look like tall humans. They can take on exact human form and people in the know say the only way to tell the difference is –' she reads from the book – 'they have a "convex rather than concave philtrum below their noses . . . "'

'Holy shit, Birta, how do you even know these words in English – convex, concave, *philtrum* . . . ?'

'When I was young and wasn't tired of people, I studied

art. Students from all over the world were at my college, and English was the common language. I was brought up learning English from the radio too; a lot of my favourite songs were in English. I also had a torrid time for a year with a Scottish man who came here to "find" himself. Instead, he found me, fucked my life up then went away again. Men are vain fools but he was an intelligent fool and lent me some great books, which were in English. I learned a lot about a lot in that year and reading books in English really hones my vocabulary. I also love English movies from the forties and fifties. I'm a strange woman.'

'You're a legend. I was listening to people speaking Icelandic yesterday and thinking how I probably couldn't learn even conversational Icelandic without about twenty years' practice. The way it sounds and is written is beautiful but completely impenetrable for me, I reckon. Anyway, the *Huldufólk* . . . Oh, wait a minute, I've remembered where I heard that before. *Hoodoo Funk*!'

Birta looks clueless.

'The dream I was just telling you about, I could have sworn as I was dropping off to sleep I heard Frank say "*Hoodoo Funk*". I was trying to work out what the hell he meant. Maybe it was "*Huldufólk*".'

'Who's Frank?'

Oops. She doesn't know about my dead but very much still here friend Frank.

'Just a friend.'

'A dead friend.'

'Erm . . . Well, yes.'

'We have a lot to talk about, you and I. Little did I know

as I shone my torch on you this morning that I would find someone so extraordinary. I think your friend was almost definitely saying *Huldufólk*. It seems you have a watcher while you're in Iceland; you mustn't be afraid. If he meant you harm, you'd know about it.'

'That doesn't sound as comforting as I think you meant it to be. So you believe in the *Huldufólk* yourself?'

'I think they're the manifestation of the souls of the rocks and trees. They live in caves, and among the rocks. They don't like anyone encroaching on their homes or land, but there are many, many stories of them saving people's lives around here. Why wouldn't I believe? The alternative is an empty world where everything is as it looks. Who on earth wants to live like that?'

'Not me!' I raise my coffee cup in a salute.

Birta turns the book around to show me a pencil drawing, in the Arthur Rackham style, of a tall long-haired shadowy figure with staring eyes and a linen-looking shirt and trousers. It's not exactly what I saw but close enough to give me a shiver.

'Bloody hell. I've never seen anything about the "Hidden Folk" before but that's pretty much it, looks-wise. I have to say, when I've spotted him out of the corner of my eye, plus when I encountered him in my dream, his energy was held back and hidden from me. But I sense that underneath the surface pulses such ancient wisdom and knowledge, being exposed to it might blow my tiny mind. This picture is flat. Those beings certainly aren't.'

Birta's eyes shine.

'Amazing. I never meet anyone like you. Or like me. Let's go to the living room and have a *Brennivín* in front of the fire. You need to get a true taste of Iceland. You obviously came to my homeland for a reason. Let's find out what it is.'

THE BLACK DEATH

Turns out *Brennivín* is completely bloody disgusting. You drink it as a shot, though, so the horror is soon over. I know other people might like it but I absolutely don't. Apparently its nickname is 'the Black Death', because of the label it used to have, black with a skull on it. I absolutely agree with the nickname and will never put it near my face again. Birta looks at me with a twinkle in her eye after I tell her I'd rather finish the bottle of red we brought with us.

'Okay, so *Brennivín* isn't for you. How about the national dish of Iceland? Men eat it to prove they're an alpha.'

'This worries me. Men do ridiculous shit to prove themselves. What are you going to subject me to?'

'I know this sounds mad but I can't serve it in here. I need to give it to you in the kitchen.'

'What? It's not like Stinking Bishop cheese, is it? I love that stuff but you can't eat it in the house. It tastes of creamy deliciousness but smells like all hell.'

'Actually, yes, very similar. Put your coat on and we'll have some near the open door. I'd be very interested in what you think. I've kept it in the outhouse where I do my pottery. In a sealed jar.'

I'm now very curious. I absolutely love smelly cheese. Has Iceland got a special one that I don't know about? I'd love to find an extra cheese to worship.

So I go to the kitchen with my coat at the ready. The open back door has already destroyed most of the warmth from the oven. But there's birdsong and breeze and snowy sunshine. It's stunning. Birta enters with a little blue pottery bowl. In it are a few small white squares of something. I step closer to get a better look and the stench is something else. It smells of ammonia. Like a very strong cleaning product, or a back lane that's been used as a toilet by five hundred drunks. I cannot believe that she thinks I would eat this stuff.

'People usually eat a cube of this then wash it down with *Brennivín* but you don't like that so you can have a glass of water.'

She hands me a toothpick. 'If you hold your nose for the first bite, you get the flavour and not the smell.'

'Birta, this is already foulness personified and I've not even tasted it yet.'

'Come on, don't be a fraidy-cat.'

'Pour me a glass of that wine.'

She does so. I spear a little square with the toothpick and hold my breath. I have no wish to elongate the agony here, so I quickly pop it in my mouth and chew. It's like cheese in consistency but meatier. I allow myself a small breath of air and for a second am relieved to find the flavour is weird but not terrible. I swallow. Then the aftertaste kicks in. My mouth and throat fill with the overwhelming flavour of pissy mattress and rotting corpse. I've never actually eaten a rotting corpse, obviously, but I just know that this is what it would taste like. Birta, I notice, doesn't take a cube herself. I begin to boke uncontrollably at this point. I'm making horrifying noises, as an extra pint of saliva floods my mouth in readiness for a huge upchuck of vomit. I put my hand over my mouth and run to the door, sucking in lungfuls of clean, freezing cold air and retching, but absolutely determined not to actually puke. It takes a few minutes before I'm fairly sure I won't be sick everywhere, then I reach my hand out and take a gulp of the wine that Birta hands me. She's laughing so hard, she has tears in her eyes, the absolute WITCH.

'What the actual fuck did you just feed me?'

She motions me back to the table and closes the back door, leaving the bowl of fetid nightmares outside on the step. She takes my hand, the one not clutching a wine glass, and warms it between her own palms for a few seconds.

'That was *Hákarl*. Fermented Greenland shark. They let it rot for a long time to get rid of the poison. But it naturally secretes ammonia.'

'Which is why it tastes of urine, you absolute maniac!'

She's laughing her head off again, and now so am I. I just ate the worst thing on the living planet and managed not to be sick. I've outmanned the men. Iceland is *insane*.

'Why the fuck would anyone want to eat something

that tastes that horrific? It's like Stinking Bishop times a thousand.'

'Proves your strength.'

'Only a man would think eating something stupid that needs to rot to get rid of poison is proof of strength. It's actually proof of being mentally unstable.'

'To be honest, only old people with less of a sense of smell and tourists eat it. I don't like to have it around, because the sharks take one hundred and fifty years to reach sexual maturity and live to be four hundred, so why would anyone kill them? But an old friend came by and brought some as a joke. I wouldn't touch it ever.'

'But you'd give it to me. You're evil.'

'You should be proud of yourself. You didn't spit it out and you kept it down.'

The aftertaste is still appalling so I keep on drinking the wine. Birta joins me. 'You're now an honorary Icelander!'

'Why, thank you.'

Suddenly I think of Milo being so freaked out last night and remember I need to charge my phone. How the hell did I forget that? I pull out my charger and realize I don't have the adapter plug.

'Birta, you don't have an adapter plug, do you? Or an iPhone charger with the right plug on it? My phone's out of juice. I've brought it over with the wire but not an adapter.'

'I'm so sorry. I don't have an adapter or any phones here. I used to have a landline but it broke.'

'You don't have a *phone*? Of any description?'

'No. Nor a TV. Just a projector with a roll-down screen.'

'Wow. What if you get injured or have a medical emergency?'

'So be it. But it's not going to happen. I'm strong as an ox.'

She stands and motions me to the living room.

'Let's get close to the fire. Tell me about this fool you followed here. I think it's right that you can't phone him. He left you here alone, I already don't like him.'

We sink into two slightly beaten-up but comfortable chairs with crocheted blankets over the backs. She puts extra wood on the fire and it begins to roar and crackle. I love it.

'What did you say his name is?'

'He's called Einar. And I think he may not be quite who he says he is. My friend Milo already hates him. I was giving him the benefit of the doubt, but I sent him a message last night when the lights went out and by six a.m. he'd still not replied. He knew I was snowed in, why wouldn't he check on me before bedtime?'

'So what did you see in him in the first place?'

'He's very tall and charismatic, and also really brilliant at what he does.'

'How he looks is all very well, but how do you know he's brilliant at what he does? What's his job?'

'He's the star of the company he works for. Computers, he says. He travels around doing stuff, I don't completely know what.'

It hits me as I talk that I don't really know much about him at all.

'Okay. So he says he's a big shot and he's charming. The first sign of a fantasist by the way, big charisma.'

'Don't say that, Birta, it just makes me feel even more stupid.'

'Oh, don't be so hard on yourself. I guarantee you, whoever he is, he won't be anywhere near as ridiculous as the men I attracted into my life. Until I stopped having any men in my life at all. How's the sex?'

'We only had sex for the first time when I arrived. And I was pretty hyped up so it was marvellous. Though it could have lasted longer, now that I think about it.'

'You flew out here to meet up with a man you'd not even had sex with?'

'We'd had a night together before that. A lot of naughtiness but no *actual* sex.'

Birta screws up her nose and shakes her head. 'You really are a total romantic.'

'I'm not sure I am. I truly did come here intending to write something, or thought I did. But so far I've eaten loads of cakes, drunk too much, read a romance novel and let my head obsess over a bloke I hardly know. Another one of my crazy mistakes.'

'We all make mistakes. And I think you've been saved by the power cut and the snow, I really do. Some perspective. Plus, you met me.'

She grins and I smile woozily back. Wine and poisonous shark meat plus the roaring fire have had an anaesthetic effect on my mind.

'I want to know about your dead friend, Tanz. The one who said "*Huldufólk*". There's more to you than you're admitting. I certainly don't think you've been completely honest about last night. You couldn't have heard the wind because there wasn't any. You need to tell me your story, fellow spooky woman. I can guarantee I'll love it.'

So, in this wild and wondrous house in the middle of nowhere, in a far-away land, I spill a bunch of beans to my new witchy friend.

TIME IS TICKING

I wake up with a heavy head. Who the hell drinks at breakfast time apart from British people at airports? After chatting for quite a while with Birta, I obviously nodded off for an hour or so. I know roughly how long I've been asleep because there's a wind-up clock on the mantelpiece, which doesn't rely on electricity to let me know the time. Sometimes vintage really is better. As I sit up, the crochet blanket still draped over my shoulders, I realize I didn't dream anything, which makes a nice change. I look around me. I'm alone in the room. The fire is lower but not out, the window shows no new snow falling outside, and the scent of incense and wood smoke is comforting.

Though the room is homely, with its book-lined walls, accommodating furniture, welcoming fireplace and thick rugs, it occurs to me that I may not be as suited to off-grid living as I imagined myself. Many a time I've dreamed of glorious solitude, but now I'm here I don't think I'd do well with no TV, phones or contact with other people. This kind of living is, for me, a short break thing. I've suddenly got a yearning for Inka, my cat, plus I want to talk to Sheila about how daft I've been, flying here on a man-whim, and tell her how I may be having yet another mid-life crisis. All at once it becomes urgent to me that I should get back to Einar's cabin, and hopefully charge my phone up, seeing as I was stupid enough to forget the adapter. I mean, how long can a power cut last? It must be sorted by now, right?

Thoughts begin to pile up in my head, then suddenly I get a hollow feeling in the middle of my brain and a pressure in my ears like I'm swimming underwater. Everything goes still and all I hear is a quiet whooshing. Then that fades and I'm listening to the clock, the one on the mantelpiece. It goes from a gentle ticking to a louder clanking, to sounding like the swinging pendulum of a large grandfather clock. It occurs to me, in a far-off way, that I can't move. I'm hypnotized and paralysed by this loud ticking in the room, as well as a creeping dread that I don't understand. A feeling that everything is 'wrong' and that time is running out. I have no idea where these feelings are coming from but they're oppressively real. Just as mute fear starts to creep into panic, Birta walks into the room. I hear a distant 'hello', then the spell breaks and everything goes back to normal. I suck in a huge relieved breath and try to seem composed in front of my new friend, who's looking rather concerned.

'Tanz. Are you okay? You've gone a funny colour.'

'Yes, sorry, I think I just had one of those half-awake/half-asleep experiences. That's what happens when you drink wine all day after a terrible night's sleep. Is the electricity back on?'

Birta shrugs. 'Not yet, no, but this is unusual. I think it'll be sorted very soon.'

I concentrate on steadying myself and smile at her.

'Right. Well, I really feel I should go back to the summer house. The snow doesn't look so thick on the ground now, and maybe Einar's had his tyre repaired. If I can't call him, I can at least be there if he shows up.'

'Okay, I'll walk you back. I have a painting I'd like to finish but I'll see you home then come over and check on you again in the morning. You may have been taken back to town by then.'

'Oh. Are you sure you don't fancy staying over?'

She looks alarmed at the prospect. Boy, she really is a lone wolf.

'Oh, no, I'm inspired to paint and I can do it by gaslight. I have several lamps and it makes the work more atmospheric.'

'Okay. Well, I'll get my boots on. I feel bad dragging you out, just for you to come back again.'

'Don't feel bad, I love wandering the countryside. Plus, when we get there you can see if you "feel" anything more of the lady that was crying. My witchiness is different to yours, I can't tune in like you can, but I can put a protection around you before I go. To be honest, I think you're very protected anyway, but a little extra can't hurt you.'

KISS

Once we get there it's immediately apparent that the power still isn't back on in the cabin. The walk was bracing but my feet are bloody cold and Birta gets the wood burner going for me while I light candles as the sky darkens. Again. I can't believe the way the light works here. I've spent a whole night at Einar's place, been to Birta's, come back and it's getting dark again. It's crazy, like I'm living in an upside-down universe where time's gone mental. I feel like I've been here a week already. I'm a tad disappointed to see that Einar's car isn't here and from the unruffled snow on the driveway it's obvious that no one has been here at any time today. But that's okay, the snow hasn't got worse, it's not that thick and I'll be back in town as soon as the electricity comes back on and I can get even the tiniest bit of juice in my phone.

Birta produces a flask out of the small tapestry backpack she's brought and I chuckle when I see that even that is an old-fashioned orange and cream. This woman is a walking vintage fashion accessory. She holds it up and grins at me.

'I made my special moss tea!'

'You absolute star.'

'We'll have a cup each, you can wander around and make sure you feel safe, then I'll go.'

The taste is earthy and slightly bitter, but with a tiny hint of something more aromatic. I like it.

'Thank you, Birta, this is weirdly comforting.'

She smiles and sits next to me on the sofa. She puts her arm around my shoulder and kisses me on the cheek. I turn to thank her for everything she's done for me and she kisses me again, very lightly on the mouth. She smoked a roll-up on the way here and has a smell of heavy aromatherapy oils to her. It's a heady mix. I didn't expect this at all and am not sure what to do. She then lifts her cup in a salute and I do the same back, feeling colour flood my cheeks. Do Icelandic women kiss each other like this? Am I reading too much into an innocent act of friendship? I get up.

'I'm going to check upstairs. I'm much braver when you're here.'

I'm not strictly lying, I do feel braver with her around, but also, bloody hell, I need to take a minute outside the room. There's just something about this woman. She exudes an attractiveness that's totally unique. Her voice is almost masculine, her energy is thoroughly feminine and she is completely her own person, sure of herself and answering to no one. I want to be like her when I grow up, though knowing my insecurities and ego, that might be never.

At the top of the stairs, I take the deepest of breaths in an attempt to calm my blushing cheeks and confused mind, then I look in on 'my' bedroom. I feel nothing scary or oppressive in here at all. Again, I get the sense it's safe and 'protected'. I determine to light the burner up here as soon as Birta leaves, so that it's all warm and comfy, then I'll bring my notebook upstairs with some nice bits of food and wine and write notes. I don't have a full idea for a story or script yet, but there's certainly enough going on at the minute for me to come up with some initial thoughts. And that will once again help with the ever-growing embarrassment that I flew all the way here for a stupid man, who couldn't even be arsed to text and see if I was okay before my phone lost the last of its power.

Back downstairs, Birta is packing away her flask.

'All well up there?'

'Yup, no bad feelings at all.'

'Do you want me to check outside with you?'

'No, that's fine. To be honest, if there's going to be any spooky shenanigans, they usually don't show themselves until I'm alone. Or with my friend Sheila, who sees ghosts all of the time.'

She stares at me, then shakes her head and chortles.

'Your life is quite incredible. I hope you appreciate how privileged you are, and enjoy it.'

'Oh, I do, mostly. I also do the odd dangerously ridiculous thing that nearly gets me killed. I'm a total liability sometimes, but mostly grateful for everything.'

'Okay, well, I will get going before it's completely dark, though I do have my torch, so it's not really a problem.'

She steps forward and I catch my breath. But she doesn't kiss me this time, she wraps me in a hug. Her hair smells of night-time forests. To my horror, I'm very aware of her breasts pressed against me through the swirly jumper she's wearing. I'm absolutely appalled by the sexual turn my thoughts have taken; I'm pretty sure that I flew here with the sensibilities of a horny goat and now am carrying that naughtiness around with me like a magma-hot satchel. I just hope Birta doesn't feel it, I don't want to embarrass the poor lass. Misconstruing someone's friendliness for sexual intent is so crass.

With coat on and hood up, Birta grins at me at the front door.

'You will be fine tonight, I can feel it. I just put a protection around you when we hugged. Also, you're a brave woman. I admire you greatly.'

'Wow. Thank you. I admire you more.'

'See you tomorrow, if that fool doesn't show up to take you away. Thank you for a fun day.'

'I'll be back at yours with a charger and an adapter if the power doesn't come back on by morning. And thank you for the rancid shark, you absolute fucker.'

Her laugh is full-throated.

'I love it when you swear. It sounds much better in your accent than any other accent I've heard.'

'Praise indeed! Be careful getting back.'

'Oh, don't worry about me, nothing can touch me. Goodnight.'

'Goodnight.'

I close the door and I'm alone again. Only I'm not alone, and I'm pretty sure it's only a question of time before I'm reminded of it. I may as well make myself comfortable before anything kicks off.

BED OF SECRETS

I bloody love this bed. It's comfortable and firm, and nestling under the covers with the fire going and candles lit, plus my notebook open ready to receive new words, I feel like a modern-day Emily Brontë. It's the Icelandic version of being a feisty woman in a draughty house on the moors. (It's not draughty in the slightest by the way, but you get what I'm saying.) On second thoughts, though, after the craziness of last night, I'm probably more like Mary Shelley, alone on a winter's night waiting for a monster to arrive.

I actually just managed to write something. It's a very short story about a ghostly woman in the snow. I didn't know how to end it, so I made it all a bit gothic and dreamy. I absolutely know this is not going to be my best work. It's not got any gags for a start – I'm funny and life all goes a bit sideways when I get too serious. But it felt nice to put pen to paper, like I popped my writing cherry. Speaking of which, I seem to have also smashed my 'fancying a delightfully older blonde witchy woman from Iceland' cherry to smithereens. I actually don't know what's going on here but my sexual faucet has definitely overheated and now I'm just throwing out my pheromones hither and thither like molten confetti. I will never tell her the effect she had on me today, but I suspect it's all tied in with getting the screaming hots for Einar back in that bar in Hampstead after ages of confusion about what the hell I was going to do with the rest of my life. Maybe when I'm getting worried about who I actually am, my body goes into sexual meltdown.

'*Close your eyes.*'

I hear it crystal clear. That voice. Gentle. Speaking English.

'*Won't hurt you.*'

I feel a peculiar mix of scared and comforted. I hear voices, that's been clear for some time now. But this voice absolutely makes me feel safe, as does this room. Out there in the snow, not so much – it's a free-for-all of crying ghosts, 'Hidden Folk' and wandering shadows – but here in this room, despite the other-worldliness of everything, I might as well trust and close my eyes. If, however, I then feel a clammy hand touching me somewhere, I'm coming out swinging. Also, when Frank finally pops up he's going to get a piece of my mind, leaving me to handle this spooky stuff on my own.

'*Close your eyes.*'

Fuck it. I do as I'm told. I also breathe slowly and deliberately into my diaphragm so I don't have a panic attack.

Behind my eyes I find a film going on. A moving vision. I calm my breathing even more, knowing it'll help me 'see'.

A dark-haired woman, curvy, in a long grey jumper and thick black woollen-looking tights, standing in a kitchen. There are farmhouse brick walls, and an Aga, not unlike Birta's. But this looks a bit battered and chipped. I've gone back in time, I reckon, but I'm not sure how many years. The woman stirs a large, bubbling pot of food then rubs her hands together to warm them up. She opens an oven drawer and takes out a chubby loaf of bread. It's steaming hot so she must have just baked it. There's the sound of a young child crying in another room. She stops and listens. The noise halts again and she looks relieved. She has large soulful dark eyes and an expressive mouth. She looks sad, though, the sides of her mouth pulling downwards, and a pinched look to her lips.

A man enters the kitchen, walks to the pot and dips in a spoon. Blowing on it, he takes a taste. I can't see his face properly, I don't know why. He has a dark beard and he doesn't look old but apart from that, nothing. It's almost like he's pixelated. I don't think 'she' is letting me see him properly. She stands back and watches him taste the food. She's tentative and I feel her longing. Eventually she steps forward and touches his neck from behind. At first he seems to stiffen like he doesn't want the contact, but she strokes her hand down his back and pushes up against him, kissing his hair and everywhere else she can reach, including the sides of his face. Eventually he turns and kisses her back. There's something almost reluctant about how he kisses but she returns the contact with ardour; then she takes his hand and pulls at him. Now we're in a sparse bedroom. Damp on one wall, a pile of rumpled blankets on the bed. As she lies back and pulls him to her, he kisses her again, and she pulls off her dress. Virtually ignoring her body, which is fulsome and soft, with stretchmarks on her belly, he pulls down his pants and mounts her. I can't believe how little intimacy he shows this beautiful woman as she writhes beneath, happy, it seems, to get even this crumb of attention. As I watch, I suddenly feel what she's feeling. The longing, the sexual frustration, the sadness and, underneath it all, a horrible sense of dread. About what, I don't know. As he thrusts, the wails of the small child kick off again. She holds on to the man's back to distract him, but he stops, then thrusts quickly and mechanically to finish what he started, and pulls away.

Her sadness beats through me. I have no idea what's happening here, but the unhappiness radiating out of the dark-haired lady is so all-encompassing; I wish I could give her a hug. I hate to admit it as it means something not good happened to her, but I'm pretty sure it's the same ghost lass I saw crying in the bushes outside. She doesn't have a single trace of malignancy in her, not that I can tell, but she sure is blue. I wonder why she's showing me this. I decide to ask outright in my head.

'What happened to you, sweetheart? What are you showing me?'

The vision completely shuts off in my head. I hear her crying again, though. Then words. '*Where is he? Why can't I find him?*'

Whoever she's looking for, I'll do my best to help. She sounds like she's in despair. What kind of heartless cow wouldn't at least try to help?

ABRACADABRA

Downstairs it's not absolutely freezing, as the wood burner wasn't completely out when I went up to my writer's bed. I've come down for some chocolate as I need sugar. I put the large candle lantern on the table and fish my bag of treats off the counter. That vision wasn't so much spooky as just sad, such a lonely existence for her. It's not escaped my notice that sex is permeating everything at the moment. So much complication and bullshit resulting from copulation seems to be the theme of my life as well as the theme of the women around me. My friend Sheila was so mistreated by men, especially her long-term ex, that she won't even consider a relationship any more. I impetuously booked a flight here with the pheromones of a giant man in my nostrils. Birta, my new, beautiful witchy friend, lives on her own in the middle of bloody nowhere partly to escape past heartache, and some poor lass, who either lived here or nearby, seems to have died horribly after basically begging for sexual attention from the bloke she lived with. He was so mechanical in bed, it was hard to watch. And what about the dream I had, the barn, and the devastated observer? Sex and the fallout from it, everywhere I look.

I sit on the sofa, munching on a hard-centred praline, blanket over my legs, remembering that embrace in the barn. In my vision or dream, whatever it was, they were completely in tune with each other, oblivious to anything else. My mind drifts to London. I was completely in tune with Neil, my policeman, when we were having sex. It was warm and sweet and he really liked me. I just didn't feel like our lives aligned when he came into my world of creativity. Maybe a part of me is broken. Maybe a part of all of us is broken . . .

I'm ripped out of my thoughts by a godawful scream from outside the stoop door. The door's glass and I can't see anyone out there, just hear screams. A woman's screams. They're loud and anguished and I push myself back on the sofa and put my hands over my ears. It doesn't stop the noise, which leads me to believe they're also in my head. I try to breathe calmly but then the knocking starts. Every single window in the room begins to bang, like a bunch of feral teenagers have descended on the place and are trying to frighten the fucking life out of me. But there's nothing. No living person is out there. I begin to scream along with the woman. Now the banging skips from one window to the next and I hear a child crying. There's also banging on the stoop, stamping on the wood, getting louder and louder. And then whomp. One last bang and silence.

'FRANK!'

I scream for him out loud. There are tears running down my face and I've dribbled chocolate down my jumper. How is anyone supposed to be okay after a display like that?

'Frank. Please, talk to me. I'm really fucking scared.'

To my relief, I hear his voice.

'*You're okay, Tanz. Go back upstairs.*'

'Why?'

'*It's a safe, protected room, it'll calm you down.*'

I do as I'm told. Actually, I run up there like my arse is on fire. It's warm in the room and I grab my wine, legs curled under me, back against the pillows.

'What just happened?'

'*It's an imprint of absolute horror.*'

'How do you mean?'

My heart is still hammering. That was absolutely terrible. The banging was straight out of every horror movie I've ever watched. Why do they have to be so bloody dramatic?

'*Something bad happened, something really bad involving death, and a trauma was left. There are secrets and it's time for them to come out. The lady with the dark hair, she wants you to find out the truth. She's trying to show you the best she can. This room is protected but downstairs, especially outside, it's showtime, now that she knows you can tune in. But she can't tell you yet, only show, and it's frustrating for her too. So she gets a little over-passionate. She's not trying to harm you, she's trying to get her point across.*'

'Well, if she wants my help, she needs to at least attempt to not give me an embolism. That was loud. Impressively so. Do you know what happened?'

'No. If I did, we could clear it up straight away. You're the cold case investigator, not me.'

'Since when was I elected as Columbo for the dead? I didn't volunteer for this job!'

'No, but you're a natural.'

'Fucksake. Last time I ended up nearly dying on a pub roof for sticking my nose in.'

Despite my protestations my mind is whirring. All at once I remember the other dream I had. That one with the guy looking over the edge of a cliff in the darkness, still as a stone. I had a huge sense that he was full of secrets. Was that her man? The man with the dark beard? I'm pretty sure it was. Did he kill himself after doing something to her? Is that who she's looking for? Also, the crying child. Did they die, or is that child still alive somewhere and could give me some answers? I wish I bloody knew how long ago this happened. Then I could work out how old the kid would be now. Maybe I *do* need my detective head on rather than my ghost-buster one. Something happened here, but with no car or contacts in Iceland, apart from Einar the absent, how could I even begin to explore this?

'Frank, I don't even know where to start here. WHY ME? I know no one in this country. I don't even know where to ask about who owned this land or lived around here in the past. Also, I'm trapped in a fucking power cut with no transport back to town.'

'That's about to change. And you're never without hidden guidance. You're always protected, you wouldn't be asked to intervene in this stuff if you weren't going to be given help along the way.'

'Still doesn't make the screaming and banging less scary.'

'No, but at least it gives it some context. And you were meant to be without your phone for a bit by the way, that's why you forgot your adapter. But it's all fine now. ABRACADABRA!'

I'm about to ask what the hell he's suddenly shouting at when the hall light goes on. I hop off the bed and find the whole of the downstairs lit up. The oven clock is flashing and the TV is on. I don't remember having it on when the power went out, but hey, I'll take whatever light and outside contact I can right now. I let out a whoop as I turn up the volume on an old episode of *Doctor Who*, with Icelandic subtitles. It seems strangely fitting. Tom Baker with his stripy wool scarf and curly mop of hair. I can make a hot cuppa! I can finally charge my phone! Why on earth didn't he want me to charge my phone before?

I boil the kettle for a herbal tea after plugging my phone into the charger. Frank's gone again; he loves a dramatic exit. Knowing my phone is pretty much up and running finally, and having the TV on for company, has emboldened me somewhat and I pull a blanket around my shoulders, shove on some fur-lined boot-slippers I found in the upstairs wardrobe, and before I can lose courage, drag the door open and venture out onto the stoop. It's peaceful out here. No extra footprints, no humans playing tricks on me. The cold is so absolute it's almost exhilarating, though I know I shouldn't stay out here long. I go down the two steps so there's less direct light on me from the kitchen and speak aloud.

'Whatever happened, I'll try to help, okay? I'll try to

make it right. Just don't give me an actual heart attack. Me being dead won't help!'

Just then I hear a noise. The tiniest of tinkles. It comes from the beautiful rowan tree with the red berries. I can see them in the light from the kitchen window. Each cluster has a diminishing little pile of snow on it, apart from one. One is clean like someone wiped the snow away. I get closer, mindful of the fact there's been a lot of 'activity' by this magical tree. Something is sparkling in the light and it isn't snow. I reach out my hand and, to my absolute surprise, I find a small bell tied by a red silk ribbon hanging over the berries from a twig. I hold it up to the light. It's silver and it emits the most musical of wee chimes.

I look around, but see no one who could have left it there. Then a voice, sonorous, calm and as far as I can tell male, speaks to me from behind the tree. Clear, precise and accented.

'A gift. For you.'

I can feel a presence suddenly, as the third eye in my forehead springs open like a trapdoor. For all I know this being has been with me all the time since I got to the cabin. Sometimes you don't notice things until they're signposted. I hold my breath and listen intently to the silence. I'm in the presence of something I've never had the honour of experiencing before. Something or someone 'other'. I want them to stay a while, I want to communicate with them, and I don't want to scare them off. I speak quietly, with reverence.

'Thank you. It's beautiful.'

There's nothing for a moment then I hear one more word.

'Chosen.'

All at once I know he's stepped back. The energy from him is like nothing I've ever felt. It's hard to detect until he pulls back and then its absence is devastating. I return to the kitchen, closing the door behind me, clutch the bell against my heart and cry big fat tears. I'm moved beyond words and not sure why. I suspect that deep down I've always wanted to know that this sometimes incredible, often extremely lonely planet has more magic going on than anyone can see or explain. And I just had proof. Most of the population wouldn't believe me, but I don't care. Personal proof. And it's blown my mind.

MILO IS NOT HAPPY

My tears abate almost as quickly as they come, but my heart has an extra element to it. A warm secret it didn't have five minutes ago. I was feeling out of control before, and scared, afraid of my own feelings as much as anything else. But now, there is a new knowledge. I've experienced the unexplained close up. True hidden magic.

Just then my phone pings. I wipe my eyes, though stray sobs are still threatening, and pick it up to look. The number of waiting texts is impressive. The one that just came through completely shocks me, an Einar special.

Tanz, darling, I'm so sorry about the power cut. I'm sure it will be sorted within a short time. I tried to call you but suspect your phone needs charging. I was flown out of the country for a meeting today but will be back soon. Happy writing! Will try to call again when I land.

How does that bloody idiot think I can get back to civilization if he leaves the country? Didn't even offer to send someone to pick me up. He didn't ask me when I'm flying back to London or anything. Now I'm starting to wonder if he's an actual psychopath. I note, as I'm thinking this, that there are multiples of missed calls from Milo showing on my screen. I reckon he must be frantic and I'm just thinking I should text him when his name flashes up and the phone rings.

'Hi, Milo.'

'Hi, Milo? *Hi, Milo?* Are you okay?'

He sounds beside himself.

'I am. I'm so sorry, the power just came back on ten minutes ago.'

'You've been stuck in the middle of nowhere with no power for twenty-four bastard hours? Also, you waited *ten minutes* to call me?'

'I'm so sorry, sweetheart. It's been off the scale mental here. It's definitely haunted just outside the cabin; I saw a sobbing woman in the bushes. Plus, a lovely lass called Birta came and rescued me this morning. She's an artist. She lives in this dilapidated but cool place half a mile away. We had wine for breakfast and she fed me rotting, fetid shark. I also think I fancy her but she's a woman, so I don't know what to make of that. Then I came back here and wrote a short story, then got even more haunted by the screaming, knocking dead woman.' I miss out the bit about getting an enchanted bell from a magical being. I want to keep that for myself for now.

'Erm, did that all really happen or did you get a knock on the head?'

'All true, scout's honour.'

He's calming down, I can tell. I hear something being poured.

'Right, I'm having a medicinal Merlot now, seeing as I've been demented with worry and you left it a FULL TEN MINUTES to let me know you were okay. And what about that gigantic fuckwit that you went there to see? Has he shown up yet?'

'No, he apparently had to fly somewhere today for a meeting and he'll be back soon.'

'Oh my God. He sounds like the single most dangerously irresponsible, uncaring man-baby EVER. And I thought I'd dated enough of that category to have met the worst of them. Please tell me you're coming home asap?'

'Of course I'm coming home but my first job is to get back into town, then I have to make some enquiries. I can't really leave until I find out what happened to the woman who's trying to reach me. She's in torment and I'm the only one who can hear her. I must be or she'd have communicated all of this to someone else who stayed here before, instead of chucking it all on me.'

'Are you kidding me? You're not the Geordie Mother Teresa of the spirit world, you know. You don't have to save all of them. Just you remember, you'll already be traumatized by Einar abandoning you like that. Plus, you can't afford to stay in Reykjavík any longer than the one night you already did. I looked up the prices, it's like going to bloody Disneyland.'

'Awwwww, were you thinking of coming over to save me?'

'Of course I was. I was so worried, I nearly booked a flight today but then I started hyperventilating. I bloody hate flying. And people. And hotels. Also, how the HELL would I have gone about finding you, even if I did come over there?'

'That's so sweet. And if it makes you feel any better, Frank says I'm being looked after and protected, so nothing terrible will happen to me.'

'*FRANK?* You mean, the Frank that led you into desperate peril with a bloke who had murdered and gutted his girlfriend upstairs? That Frank? Or the Frank that led you to almost certain death with a knife-wielding, blanket-wearing lunatic?'

Okay, so this shouldn't be funny, but his tone is so deadpan that I begin to giggle.

'What are you laughing at? It's like the blind leading the blind here. It's like every time I speak to you there's some terrifying drama going on and you're not even that bothered. I've bitten three of my nails down to the quick since yesterday. And they're my toenails!'

'I'm so sorry, Milo, I'm not laughing at you. You just have this amazing ability to make a horrible situation feel all right again.'

'Do I?'

Immediately he sounds touched. Milo has no idea how important and incredible he is, or how happy it makes me to even know him.

'Of course you do. That's why you're my best friend.

Oh, I've just had a thought. Do you mind if I make a call and I'll ring you right back? I have an idea how I can get out of here.'

'Now you're talking. Call me back soon, though, do you hear? I can't have you going off radar like that. It knocks me sick.'

'Of course. Speak soon. Love you.'

Upstairs in the room I now think of as 'my' room, the gorgeous glass electric lamp is illuminating the place serenely, the heating has put itself back on, and I'm searching through my bag for something. I didn't put it in my purse, I put it in the middle flap somewhere but I can't remember exactly where. Then suddenly I find it. A small piece of paper with a number neatly written on it in blue biro. And a name. Thor.

To my surprise, he picks up on the second ring. It sounds like he's in a pub.

'*Halló.*'

'Thor, hello! It's me, Tanz. You dropped me at my hotel when I landed a couple of days ago. I'm the Geordie lass who was staying at Room With A View.'

'Of course, I remember you – you're not easy to forget!'

Bloody hell, I don't know if he's being sweet, ironic or another silver-tongued swine.

'Well, I'm sorry to bother you but I'm in a bit of a pickle.'

'Just a minute, let me go outside.'

There's a lot of fumbling and a bunch of loud talking as he evidently pushes past people to leave the pub.

'Hey, sorry, took a bit of negotiating but I finally escaped! So what's happened?'

'I'm in a cabin, a summer house about an hour from Reykjavík centre, and I got snowed in last night, then there was a power cut. The man who dropped me here has gone AWOL and I don't know if it's possible to pay anyone to come and get me or even if the roads are passable enough, but I'd like to get back to town tomorrow morning. And also find somewhere to stay tomorrow night that won't cost too much.'

'Tanz, were you taken there by Einar, by any chance?'

Holy mackerel, he could have said almost anything and he says that. How the hell could he know?

'Erm. What the fuck! How . . . ?'

'Einar is a friend of mine. Everyone knows Einar. And that's not his place, it's mine.'

'It's WHAT?'

'My parents owned it, now it belongs to me and my sister but she lives in Amsterdam. He has a key. I'll explain when I see you. I don't know why you'd think you're snowed in, this snowfall is nothing compared to what we usually get. It's no match for my winter tyres. Will you be okay tonight? I can come and get you first thing, no charge? I'd come now but I've had six doubles; I can hold my drink but I can't lose my licence because of my job.'

'Wow, no. Tomorrow morning would be great, if you're sure? I'm fine for now. Plenty to eat and drink. Just a bit weirded out.'

'I don't blame you, you got trapped on your own. Sleep well. See you in the morning.'

'See you. And thank you so much.'

'You're welcome.'

Jesus, I wasn't even snowed in, I was simply dumped. Einar really is just a massive bellend.

I look through a pile of DVDs, on a shelf underneath the records. There's no way I'm going to sleep any time soon after today's excitement. I'll put something light and funny on and try to relax instead. (And if any more banging starts, I'll kick off.)

I clutch my little bell close and lie back on the sofa. Better to dwell on magical beings and their special energy than get more upset over that poor depressed ghost, or that very much alive shithead who dumped me here and left the country. What an absolutely crazy couple of days. When I get back to my flat in Crouch End I'll probably kiss the carpet. That is if Inka hasn't shat all over it as a protest that I left her. The thought makes me giggle. What a life.

SUCH AN IDIOT

It's still dark outside when I hear a car pulling up. It's 9 a.m. and I slept much better than expected, though I still woke a few times, so my eyes are stinging a bit. I don't remember dreaming and I had a lovely cuppa an hour ago with the doors open, listening to whatever birds were outside, already feeling the relief of escape. I absolutely knew Thor wouldn't let me down. And seeing as nothing's felt sure over the past couple of days, that was such a comfort. Some people are just legends who mean what they say.

Before nodding off last night I waded through my messages, which was no mean feat, I can tell you. I couldn't say anything to little mam as she doesn't do texts, just phone calls, so I'll have the joy of explaining what's going on very soon via a call or I'll be right in the shit. I had five missed calls from her, so I reckon she's already picked up on the fact that I'm on some kind of spooky adventure. I already spoke to Milo so that was fine. More texts from Neil prompted me to message him with:

Sorry, lad, ran off to Reykjavík to try and do some writing. Will call you as soon as I'm back.

I think the least I can do is chat with him. I really did just leave him hanging, didn't I? My big concern right now is that I'll be running off from Birta this morning without saying goodbye. I can't call her or anything, so she's not going to know where I am. After all of her amazing help and company, plus the horrifically funny 'culture' lesson, it feels absolutely terrible just going away without a word. She said she would call back round here today, but she also said she was going to paint something last night, so she may have stayed up for hours and won't be up for ages yet. My feelings for her are so confusing. It's like I've known her for years but don't know her at all. She's an addictive, clever woman who I'd like to hang out with more. I decide I'll write her a note and tape it to the front door so she doesn't miss it.

I also got a message from Sheila asking if I'm okay. She got a more comprehensive reply than most as she's usually my ghost-busting partner. Her response at seven o'clock this morning is still blowing my mind.

An idiot, a lady love and a bell. Use your instincts, sweetheart. You've got this.

Holy FUCK, how does she do it? I said nothing about my tree gift, and not much at all about Birta. I'm so proud to be mates with a true clairvoyant. I'm still mulling this message over when the front door opens and in walks Thor with a worried smile, carrying a paper bag. His face is lovelier than I remember. He's got the kindest eyes, with crow's feet and a well-cut reddish beard. He hands me the bag.

'Best almond croissants in Reykjavík. Should we have them before we go back?'

Coffee is made and I hug this stranger with so much gratitude in my heart. We sit and eat as he talks.

'I think I need to explain some stuff about Einar, just so you get it.'

'Okay.' These words make me feel extremely nervous, partly because I think a dream bubble is about to be truly burst, and partly because I'm very embarrassed about my behaviour.

'So first of all, he is the most charming man in the world so don't feel bad he got to you.'

Bingo. One sentence in and tears are rolling down my cheeks. He pushes on.

'Einar had a horrible childhood. His mum was a self-obsessed woman who always made herself the victim. And his dad was crazy as shit. He practically lived with us from age sixteen, because my parents really liked him, but by then a lot of the damage was already done. And now, he has a girlfriend from Denmark who comes over once a month but he just can't settle.'

'Oh fuck!'

Thor looks at me quizzically. 'What?'

'When I flew in he spent a little while at my hotel then ran off. When I asked why, he said his flatmate needed to talk to him overnight as he had a horrific, needy girlfriend from Denmark.'

'Einar has no flatmate. He inherited a small apartment from his grandfather. I'm surprised he hasn't sold it yet, or lost it in a bet. His girlfriend stays there when she's here. But he really does make her life impossible; I think she only stays with him because she's as crazy as he is. And I know where he was two nights ago. He messaged me from the casino. Einar likes to gamble.'

'You're kidding?!'

'That's where all his money goes. He's in debt so badly.'

'But he buys the best champagne and was staying in a stunning flat in London.'

'Yes, his friend owns a flat in London. Look, I'm sorry to upset you, but she's his lover too. She travels with work. She must have been away when you two met. She lets him have the place when he pops over. The company he works for will get him hotels but they're not swanky enough. Einar has to have the best, he can't help it. And the money he's always flashing isn't his, it's borrowed. He really doesn't mean to upset people, Tanz. He wants to show everyone a good time and he wants to have fun. It's just who he is.'

'Wow, so he's a conman?'

Thor looks abashed. He has such a healthy, ruddy face and a great bone structure, I hate bringing sadness to him and messing with his happy twinkle.

'Not quite. He's a mess, he's damaged and he falls for women on the spot. But he truly does think he loves them, in the moment. And if he invited you over here, he must have really liked you, that wouldn't be a con. It was impetuous and risky but he will have meant it at the time. Einar doesn't think about consequences. And I know that Lina must have smelled a rat because she turned up the day before yesterday with very little warning. Did he suddenly leave you before lunchtime?'

'Yes, he did.'

'She dropped in on him from the sky. Texted ahead then showed up for lunch and a bust-up. He's been in crisis talks with her ever since. Though not really crisis because she always takes him back.'

'Oh shit, I'm such an idiot.'

Thor puts his hand on my arm and shakes his head. 'You aren't an idiot, you're someone who follows your heart. When you got in my minibus I could feel the life pulsing through you. Then when you talked about staying in a summer house I did wonder. I don't want you to be sad, Tanz, but this isn't the first time he's done this.'

'Oh fuck, really?'

'He has his own key. He hides here when life gets too much. He's also used it as a short-term love-nest in the past because Lina doesn't come here. It's his escape. I'm sorry, Tanz. He's a broken person but he means no harm.'

'But he left me here, Thor. He told me he flew out of the country for a meeting yesterday. Completely lied out of his back teeth.'

'I don't think he would have known what to say to you once Lina showed up. I also don't think he set out to hurt you, and to be perfectly honest, when he offered you a place to come and write, the chances are he didn't think you were such a daring person that you'd say yes there and then and fly over. You have to remember he loves to impress. He probably thought it would make him sound cool and you would be addicted to him, so he could make love to you next time you were in London. You called his bluff.'

I love the way he says 'make love to you'. So old-fashioned and sweet. The rest of what he just told me makes me feel mortified and ashamed. I obviously know nothing about men at all. I need to be so careful. My radar is a bin fire.

'Thor, have you had to miss work to come here?'

'No, my friend Gunnar is skint at the moment and I'm not, so I gave him two days' worth of my shifts. It feels nice to be off the leash, to be honest. I think I should give you the tour you should have had, if Einar had behaved. Let's lock up and get you back to town.'

'Can I just say, this place is absolutely wonderful and thank you so much, even if you didn't actually agree to me staying here?'

'Oh, you're welcome. I'm glad you like it.'

'I've tidied up as much as possible and made the bed. But I didn't wash the sheets, sorry. I didn't know if anyone would be around to get them out of the machine.'

'It's fine. It all looks pretty good to me. You ready to go back to town? I've got you somewhere to stay. Remember, I'm also a tour guide, and a friend who is away got no takers on renting her place out. She gave me the key to look after it. It's yours. On me.'

'Wow, Thor, you don't have to go to all that trouble, that's above and beyond.'

'Oh yes I do. I don't want you thinking all Icelandic men are unreliable. Einar's just troubled.'

He stands and picks up my little case on wheels.

'Come on then. Let's get you back to streets and people!'

He doesn't have to say it twice.

ACCIDENTAL TOURIST

Thor's 'car' is a four-wheel-drive Jeep and the snow seems to mean absolutely nothing to it, as we whizz along the mostly empty roads. Thor is not a tall man, he's probably just a couple of inches taller than I am, but he has such an easy assurance about him, you can't help but feel safe.

'Thor, how does someone as capable as you are remain such good friends with a big ball of chaos?'

He laughs heartily at this and offers me a mint from a little tin, then takes one himself.

'I knew Einar at school. I don't like to reinforce stereotypes but we really are a small population in Iceland and around Reykjavík, people are either related or they have friends in common. Not everyone likes everyone, but in Einar's case, I've known him a long time and he still makes me laugh. As you may have noticed we have a very healthy drinking culture here, and no one is more fun than him when he's drunk. He just tends to take it further than everyone else. He's a big guy so he can take a lot of alcohol, plus the cocaine helps him stay up all night.'

'*Cocaine?*'

'Oh yes, of course. You cannot drink as much as he does and stay awake and functioning almost every day and night without at least a bit of "help". I think that's why he gets himself into so much trouble these days. The coke has fried his brain somewhat.'

'Oh my GOD, Thor, how the living fuck did I not see that straight away?'

'Because he's *charming* and *fun* and says the right things. Did you come here thinking you guys would be a couple?'

I suck on my mint thoughtfully. These Icelandic lads are very direct.

'I don't know, you know. I sort of had someone at home, but Einar made me feel free. It was all a bit dangerous and spontaneous. I'd begun feeling stale, so . . .'

'So he reflected what you wanted right back at you. Danger and spontaneity in someone you just met is all very well but that's all you're going to get. Late nights and passionate arguments get really fucking boring after a while, when maybe you just want to chat with your person and eat some food and make love then go to sleep. Einar doesn't sleep. That's when his demons come.'

'Jesus. First off, what a shitty, knackering life, avoiding demons all of the time. Plus, his poor girlfriend, and all the other poor women he pulls in. Secondly, though . . . how are you so emotionally intelligent? You're a bloke.'

He shakes his fist playfully.

'Don't be sexist! I dated a narcissist when I was younger.

I watched a lot of videos on YouTube about it when I was trying to decompress from the pain and damage. They were in English and I know all the terms now. She was a "grandiose narcissist"; they're the fucking worst because they're so sexy and alluring that you get addicted. Einar's not totally that, he does have feelings for others, I promise you. It's just he runs away all of the time. I have my head screwed on, Tanz, or I thought I did, and still I fell for her messed-up charms. That's why you shouldn't beat yourself up. Some people are just not worth the anguish.'

'Woah. I now need to do some studying. This is fascinating. And you're like an accidental angel. Not that I believe in accidents.'

'No, I don't believe in them either. And I feel strongly that I owe you the trip that Einar didn't give you.'

'You don't owe me anything.'

'I now represent my country in an episode of "restore Iceland's honour".'

I shake my head at his shit joke, the early sun casting a glow over the glacier as we approach town, and Thor laughs at his own ebullient proclamations of honour restoration. Then he smiles companionably by my side and the feeling of warmth coming from him is a massive comfort.

Soon enough he's pulling into a tiny driveway outside a place that looks almost like a portacabin, painted a gritty yellow that I like. This trip is a never-ending stream of surprises. When he shows me inside, there's a little bedroom, a cute kitchen and a living room with two chairs, a fire and a small dining table for two. All painted in cheery colours and with green plants dotted everywhere. The bathroom is to the side and has a shower and loo in it. It's aqua blue and fuchsia pink. He hands me a key.

'She's away for four more days.'

'What about rent?'

'No, she's my partner's sister and uses the summer house for free. I look after this place while she's away. She'll be glad someone is in here. Just water her plants and leave her some wine; red is her favourite. Now put your case down and come on. Today is for fun. By the way, do you have a swimming costume?'

Weirdly, because I'd heard of the Blue Lagoon, I did pack a functional cossie just in case.

'Yes, why?'

'Bring it along.'

I don't argue, it's so nice to be back in the thick of things. Plus I'm still in shock that I have a free place to stay. How lucky am I? I packed the costume in a little plastic bag, because I'm always worried that I'll have to fly back with it damp and get my other stuff wet. And now there's a possibility I'll have to carry it wet today, so I'm glad I thought ahead.

'Am I allowed to know where we're going?'

'No. Let's just say we'll do all the things a tourist should do today. But with a twist. I'll show you the hidden gems.'

I give him a hug. He smells of a nice cologne and wool. His beard scratches my cheek.

'You are amazing.'

'Thank you. Now come on!'

It's while I'm putting on my seat belt that I think about Birta again and how I left without a goodbye. I hope she got my note. I put my number on there in case she ever comes into town and can use a phone. I also thanked her for saving me in my hour of need.

'Thor, do you know a lady called Birta who lives half a mile down the road from your summer house? In a slightly falling-down building?'

'No. I thought the old farmhouses were too far gone for habitation.'

'Not this one. Leaky roof and stuff but still standing. This woman is an artist and she doesn't like people. But she came and found me and we hung out yesterday. She doesn't have a phone, though. I wish I could say goodbye.'

'I only know the family who have the cabin about two miles away. The dad knew my dad. Maybe your friend is a squatter and staying quiet so she doesn't get found out.'

'I don't know about that, but she's a lovely person.'

'She might have her reasons for wanting to be anonymous.'

'Yes, I think she does.'

'Ready to be chauffeured?'

'I certainly am.'

He toots his horn jauntily as we drive off.

WATERFALL

Holy fuck, they're not big on health and safety in Iceland and I love it. Common sense or die. Thor brings me to see the Strokkur Geysir, which is a hot geyser that shoots in the air every six minutes or so and is bloody powerful. And all that separates people from the upsurge of water is a loose rope. In the UK, some stupid kid or show-off drunkard would be straight over that thing and at the edge of the danger-hole. Here, people actually behave. And it has to be said, there's something very exciting about standing close, and watching hot water shoot right up in the air, up to forty metres Thor tells me, which is a hundred and thirty feet, and rain down droplets on the observers. It's like a giant whale squirting sea spray from its blowhole. The countryside around here is mossy and snowy, the air is bracing and there's a fog descending, which adds a lot of atmosphere to an already otherworldly, ancient-looking scene (only disturbed by the many different coloured hats and coats of chilly tourists, who I stand away from because I can't be arsed with people today).

Thor winks at me.

'You like?'

'Oh, I love. Uncontrollable forces of nature are my favourite.'

'I can imagine.'

He links his arm in mine.

'We should walk around the Haukadalur Valley while we're here. Lots of hot springs and bubbling mud. Like a sci-fi movie. I'm used to these things but I love to see the visitors' faces.'

'I'm sold.'

It really is lovely wandering with Thor. He's easy-going and companionable and answers my questions like a pro. When we get back in the car he won't tell me where we're going next. After driving a while he stops at a cafe for take-away coffees and two smoked salmon sandwiches on rye bread, which he says we can have at our next destination. The destination in question turns out to be the breathtaking Gullfoss waterfall. I've never seen such a powerful body of water up close. The fog adds an extra air of mystery while we chew and listen to the water thundering down. Sitting on a mossy shelf together eating our sandwiches, I find myself trying not to cry.

'Oh no, Tanz, what's wrong?'

'Nothing's wrong. I just feel emotional. It's been such a mad few days. And this is quite a thing to see. Thank you so much.'

His eyes soften and he smiles at me from behind his beard. He really does have a lovely face.

'Thor, why are you doing this? Being so kind?'

'I told you. Righting a wrong. Plus, I like you and if you weren't taken with my idiot friend, I'd probably make an absolute fool of myself trying to woo you.'

'I thought you had a partner?'

'I do. But we have an open relationship. And if she laid eyes on you, she'd probably fancy you even more than I do.'

'Wow. I think I've led quite a sheltered life. You Icelanders definitely live differently.'

'Oh, not everybody does. This is more of a "me" thing than cultural. A lot of people here marry and have children very young. And most of them are monogamous, or say they are. I just happen to not be this time, after getting hurt so badly before. And it's my partner's choice really as she likes women too. We've not been together that long, but I thought I'd give it a go and so far it's okay, I think.'

'Wow.'

I don't know what else to say. I gnaw on my sandwich and look off into the distance, the rocky landscape just visible through the mist. My eyes are hardly focused as I allow the crashing of the water to cleanse my mind. Suddenly I jump to attention as a figure appears fleetingly on the rocks in the distance, then dematerializes again. Could it be? My hand flies to my throat as I reach inside my coat and finger the tiny bell that's now on a chain around my neck, which originally had an amethyst pendant hanging from it when I arrived. That's now in my bag, and the bell has pride of place under my jumper. I acknowledge my eyes could be playing tricks but I also *know for sure* they aren't. My heart is thumping. I've never felt anything like I feel for that 'being'. Nothing earthly covers it. He's my hero. He's proof that I don't have to survive in my lifetime believing in the lowest common denominator. I have an otherworldly friend out there in the fog and he gave me a special bell. He's not human, I've only seen him as a shadow, but he's spoken to me and he gave me a gift. It's like something from a fantasy movie and it makes me feel less alone. I also know for sure that he needs something from me. I don't know what it is yet, but I'll find out and I'll make it happen, like a quest. Because in the strangest way, he, if it is a he, has restored my faith.

'Thor, do you believe in magic?'

He searches my eyes for a joke. When he doesn't see one he shrugs.

'Why not? I'm open to all possibilities.'

'Einar told me that there was a lot of magic in Iceland and that he could harness it.'

'If Einar could harness magic, he'd magic himself out of debt. I believe in all kinds of things but I wish Einar believed in himself. He's like my brother, Tanz. My broken brother.'

There are tears running down my cheeks *again*. 'I think I'm having a controlled breakdown, Thor.'

Thor looks at me then scoots forward.

'May I hug you, Tanz?'

I don't know what to say, so I nod. He pulls me into surprisingly strong arms and nestles me into his jumper, kissing the top of my head and surrounding me with absolute safety.

'You're not having a breakdown, Tanz, you're learning and blossoming.'

'You think?'

He leans back and looks into my eyes and I swear, I don't think I've seen such honest kindness in my whole life.

'I've never, ever met anyone like you before and I just wish I'd found you before Einar did. Now, come with me, I can help you with this. I guarantee you'll feel better when we get to our next stopping place.'

I follow him. What else am I going to do?

COME BACK

Oh man, he wasn't wrong. Sitting in a 'secret' hot spring in my swimming costume, I can feel the tension draining out of me. There was a little hut to get changed in when we arrived, and Thor actually put his finger to his lips as I climbed into the small, hot pool and sat down.

'Special treat, our secret. The farmer who owns this is a little picky about who he lets in. I called him earlier and he said he'd make sure we had the place to ourselves for an hour, which was very good of him.'

Surrounded by craggy nature, with a beer in my hand (I don't usually drink beer, but who was I to say no to such a thoughtful gesture), I feel like some kind of old-school goddess. I look at Thor, who happily sits opposite, his surprisingly hairy chest showing above the waterline, as he raises his beer in a toast and grins at me. I nod my thanks.

'How lucky I met you on the way in, Thor. You've shown me what I would never have seen on my own. And you rescued me. If I believed in coincidences, I'd say this was an amazing one. But I don't, I think I was meant to meet you and you are an extraordinary human. How fucking crazy is it that you owned the summer house I was going to stay in?'

'Meant to be. I liked your spirit as soon as we met. Einar may be a fool sometimes but he has good taste.'

I feel my cheeks slightly flushing. I have to resist fancying Thor as well, even though he's interesting, has made it clear he likes me and has a very impressive chest rug. I've already thrown my knickers at a certifiable giant loon, then got hot and bothered about a wonderful hippy woman. I think my sex drive has finally left me to my own devices this afternoon and for that I'm grateful.

'Thor, is it an Icelandic thing to be so laid-back? Or is it just you?'

He squints up into the sky as a muted drizzle breaks through the misty clouds and darkening sky. I feel like a rock-monster or a troll could walk straight out in front of us right now and I wouldn't even be surprised. That throbbing of ancient drums deep inside me is greatly magnified here, and I like it. Like an extra pulse in my veins.

'I don't know about that, I have nothing to compare it to but the tourists, and they're always going to be a bit overexcited, aren't they? Let's just say I've been through enough in my life to know that remaining calm in every situation is easier and leads to much less drama. And remember, we have weather that goes from snow, to sun, to rain, to unbelievably cold, to windy as hell here, sometimes within the hour. We come from a place of extremes in weather and light. So maybe we just don't overreact to the small stuff. One thing, though, never irritate an Icelandic woman. They don't mince their words and the older they get, the less tolerant they are.'

'Good on them!' I think of my little mam who doesn't mince her words either. I really need to give her a call. And that's when I suddenly feel a tug in my solar plexus and hear a voice.

'*Come back.*'

A wispy far-away voice. The woman with the dark hair that I heard crying at the cabin.

'*Must come back.*'

She's not crying now. Her voice is far away but doesn't sound weak or broken. She sounds determined. And as she repeats it, a large stone beside my head plops into the hot, steaming water. I didn't touch the bloody thing, and Thor looks at the place it fell from, then at me, questioningly. I don't know what to do. Scaring Thor about his cabin after all he's done for me seems mean. Plus, he's going to think I'm a wrong 'un, but what choice do I have, when he's the only one with transport who can help me?

'Thor, I didn't make that rock fall off and I have something to tell you.'

His eyes light up. 'I knew it.'

'Knew what?'

'You're a magic woman. It's so obvious. You have this energy, it's quite something. I was wondering when you'd reveal it.'

'Holy fuck, I thought you were going to be scared. You *want* spookiness?'

'Of course I do. Come on, fire away.'

'This is about a ghost, Thor. We need to go back to your summer house. It's currently being haunted by a distressed woman who really needs my help. She raised holy hell the night before you came to get me. Banging the windows and all sorts. And I saw her crying outside.'

He whistles. 'Scary, but cool scary.'

'Not so cool at the time. Listen, I think my new friend Birta can help me clear her. Birta is as witchy as I am in a slightly different way. But I have to go back there to do it.'

'Amazing!' He looks so happy, like I just gave him a fantastic present.

'Did you ever see or hear anything there before?'

'No, though my girlfriend said last time we were there that she heard a little bell chiming a couple of times when she was sitting in one of the rocking chairs on the porch. When she realized there were no wind-chimes hanging anywhere she took it as a sign of good luck.'

My heart fills with such warmth at this. I'm not going to mention that part of the story to him or anyone else. That secret is mine, all mine.

'Will your girlfriend mind? You driving me about and not coming home?'

'Oh, she's fine, she's not the jealous type. And we don't live together, I mostly only stay with her on weekends. Let's do it! You can tell me more about the banging ghost on the way there.'

He seems genuinely excited and, once again, proves to be the most open of human men. Men are often harder to talk to about spooky stuff as they're hard-wired to believe in facts and hard facts only. Of course, I've met those that were happy to be persuaded that there may be 'something else' out there, but it took a bit of work. Thor, on the other hand, is now acting like an excited puppy who found out he's going to get steak for dinner.

We get dried and dressed in separate little cubicles, which is a relief, as other countries seem rather more open to mixed nudity than England and I'm not open to it in the slightest, unless naughtiness is imminent. The farmer here factored in privacy. Good man. I think back to dancing naked with Einar. I now believe that he 'harnesses' magic all right. The magic to blind people to everything but his charm. How flippin' dangerous but, also, how utterly seductive. I will be on my guard for such sorcery from now on; exciting times with an 'in the moment' hedonist are all very well, but certainly not worth the bit where you're dumped in the bin as if you never existed. I check my phone once I'm in the car. Texts and messages from the usual people that I *really* need to reply to soon. But none from Einar. Could he truly have abandoned me so completely?

'Thor, does Einar know you came to get me?'

He sighs through his nose, as he navigates us down a lane to the main road. The fog and drizzle have intensified.

'Sorry, Tanz, I should have told you. I called and left him a voicemail today seeing as he wasn't picking up. Told him he was an absolute idiot, that I knew what he'd done and that I was disappointed in him. Told him I'd made sure you're safe but to keep away as he'd caused enough damage. I rarely speak to him like that, but he went too far this time.'

'Woah. Did he get back to you?'

'Yes, "Sorry". One word, that's what he said. "Sorry." He never apologizes so that was interesting in itself. But also, he's usually got a LOT to say. He knows this is bad, what he's done. It's unfortunate timing that he got found out. And don't forget that he left you in the hotel to go to the casino on the first night. That's not polite; he was already in the wrong.'

'He really is a shit, isn't he?'

'With women, yes, he can be. However, think of it this way: if Lina hadn't shown up, you would have had a strange few days of hot and cold from him. Maybe you would have got even more addicted to him, believing his "I am a libertine!" bullshit.'

My head snaps around to look at him and I yelp a laugh.

'Wow, you know that speech?'

'Of course. Every time he's caught out with another woman or gets into trouble over a new gambling debt, he starts drinking shot after shot in Olstofa bar, declaring he has to behave like this as he's a libertine and *eighteen for ever*. Who the fuck wants to be eighteen for ever? I hated being eighteen!'

'Oh, he never told me the eighteen for ever bit. That's sad, he's older than me.'

'No one dares mention his age, he gets very grumpy.'

We stop at the intersection to the main road and it occurs to me that this fog is now looking dangerously thick. The fog lights help but I'm not sure we should drive through this for too long.

'Thor, we can go tomorrow if you like, this fog's a bit hardcore.'

As I say this, I hear the voice again . . .

'*Come, come now. Help me.*' It's even more urgent in tone and volume than the last time.

'It's up to you, Tanz, but I drive in weather like this a lot. I know it looks scary but I'll be careful and it's a good adventure, no?'

He's not wrong. And I seem to have very little choice about returning to the cabin as soon as possible.

'It is a good adventure. And I have to say, if Einar has someone like you as a friend, he can't be all bad.'

'He's not all bad, he's got a brilliant mind. But he does need a public health warning tattooed on his forehead.'

We both laugh and he pulls out, ready for our foggy drive to a crying ghost whose name I don't even know.

Just another day at the office then.

ALFVIN THE HERO

I'd rather drive through a snow-storm than blinding fog. Thor can tell I'm nervous, so he decides he's going to educate me in a little dose of Icelandic music. He puts on a CD of an old Icelandic band I've never heard of called HAM. In many ways they're heavy metal, but the lead singer sounds like an opera singer. They remind me of another band called Rammstein because of the operatics, though they're not quite as hardcore, and from what Thor tells me, their lyrics are funnier. I wouldn't know, obviously, but actually the pounding guitars work very well in this strange weather. Like I'm driving along in my very own horror film with its own pulsing soundtrack. Hopefully not to my doom, though.

Thor starts to sing along in a deep faux-operatic voice and his enthusiasm is catching. He knows the lyrics inside out. I can't help laughing. I pretend to play the drums as he sings away, but get nervous again as I see headlights behind getting rather close. It's hard to tell at first but it looks like a lorry, a big one, and I don't like how it keeps bearing down on us then slightly pulling back again. Thor checks his mirror and shakes his head.

'Absolute fool.'

He speeds up but so does the lorry. He's stopped singing now. He slows ever so slightly and flashes his lights.

'If you weren't in the Jeep, there's no way I'd let this asshole pass me.'

He slows down a little more as this monster of a truck passes by, honking its horn as it does so. Without outwardly showing any anger, I can tell that Thor is annoyed because his lips have tightened. He speeds up again so he's close to the lorry, but before I freak out at this cat-and-mouse dangerousness, I'm distracted by something up ahead. There's a car pulled off to the side of the road with its hazard lights on and there's a figure waving its arms frantically. Thor is concentrating on chasing the lorry so I grab his leg.

'Slow down, slow down, SLOW DOWN.'

He now sees the car ahead and smoothly slows. His brakes are evidently excellent.

'Pull in, please.'

I've got to hand it to him, he takes orders well and he reacts very quickly. He passes the stationary car and pulls in ten feet in front of it. Two mind-blowing things happen then, virtually simultaneously. As we pass the figure who was waving, he looks straight at me. He's shadowy and tall with long hair, and too cloaked in mist to see features, but I can't miss the eyes that shine like stars in the fog-light glare. As I'm absorbing this, there's a terrible loud bang from ahead, like the world just exploded. I've never heard anything that calamitous up close but it sounds like I imagine Armageddon would. I scream and Thor shouts something in Icelandic. We get out of the Jeep and I look behind me in the lay-by. There's no car behind us. It's gone. Someone's sped off, that's the only plausible explanation. Up ahead we can hear quite a terrible clatter. Thor looks to me, holding my arm.

'Are you okay?'

'Shaky but fine. You?'

'I'm okay but I need to go and see what's going on. Stay here.'

'Don't be fucking ridiculous, I'm not staying anywhere.'

We both walk up the road. Thirty feet ahead, we find the lorry on its side, skewed across the lanes. The silence is terrifying. It occurs to me that if we'd been behind it when it toppled, we'd have driven straight into it and probably be dead. I can see the same thought in Thor's eyes as he takes my hand and we stand there wondering what on earth to do. The driver's door, currently pointing to the sky, opens up and a man climbs out and sits atop the upturned cab. When I say man, he looks about twenty and wired to all hell. We get closer and shout to him. He looks down and waves. His face is clean-shaven and white as a ghost. He pulls out a cigarette and lights it. I can see his hand shaking from here. Considering how he was driving I'm pretty bloody impressed he had his seat belt on. There's no way he'd be climbing out of there if he hadn't. Thor steps forward and they talk for quite a long time. It's a slightly 'animated' chat, to say the least, and I'm pretty sure the lad is apologizing. He puts his hand in his back pocket, pulls out his phone, then gives a thumbs up and makes a call.

Thor listens then walks back to me.

'He says he's sorry for driving like that but his first baby is due and he was trying to get back to Akureyri in good time. The girlfriend's not in labour yet but could be any time. I told him he could have killed us and he's begged me not to tell the police exactly how he was driving because it's the only job he's good at. He's promised it was a stupid mistake and he's calling it in now to the police. What do you think?'

'About what?'

'Well, we can put a flasher and a stop sign at the side of the road back there to warn anyone who gets here before the police and carry on, or we can wait and give a statement.'

I blow on my hands. The feeling that I want to keep going is almost overwhelming but makes me feel terrible.

'Is it bad that I'd really like to press on? It's bloody freezing, we're not dead and he's okay. Can you smell petrol?'

We both sniff. There's nothing, so hopefully the rig isn't going to blow up. Thor shouts something to the lad and he scrambles down to the ground like a mountain goat, ciggie in his mouth. He approaches and speaks to Thor again. Then looks at me and in a thick Icelandic accent says, 'I'm sorry for being stupid.'

Me being me, I just see a frightened lad with shaky hands who would have been dead as a dodo right now if he'd not had his seat belt on. I grab him and give him a hug.

'We're all lucky tonight.'

He hugs me back and I can feel the fear and relief in him.

Thor runs to the Jeep and comes back with a huge woollen blanket and puts it over the lad's shoulders. He then walks off again, gets something from the boot and moves off down the road. The lad sits down on a roadside fence, blanket wrapped around his shoulders and another fag in his hand. I walk back to the Jeep, thinking I'll get in and get warm if Thor takes any length of time. I'm just by the passenger door when I hear a voice, from the darkness beyond the road. Clear, calm and not of this world.

'*Chosen.*'

I don't disturb the bell around my neck but still, I hear the tiniest of chimes. I can see nothing in the absolute blackness but I can 'feel' him. A presence that is full and empty at the same time. My heart skips and I whisper, 'Tell me your name.'

There's silence, then at last the voice again. More distant this time.

'*Alfvin.*'

I wrap my jacket closer around me and quietly repeat it back to him. 'Alfvin . . . Thank you.'

Thor emerges from the dark and goes to speak to the driver once more. As they chat, the lad's phone goes. The call lasts twenty seconds or so. Thor walks back over to me.

'Let's go.'

'You sure?'

'Yup. The police will be here imminently, that's what he was just told. He'll have to explain away the stop sign and lamp I just put back there. And the blanket. But apart from that, we're not needed. Anything we have to say would just make his life worse.'

'Okay.'

I wave at the lad and he waves back, mouthing, 'Thanks.'

'You're welcome,' I call. 'And no more driving like a fucking lunatic. You have a baby on the way.'

He nods, shamefaced. I nearly said daughter; I feel very strongly it's a little girl. But it's not my business to get into all that. He'll find out soon enough.

Thor switches the heating on full blast as we drive past the shaken driver and I can't help dwelling on how close we just came to catastrophe. Thor takes us past the lorry by carefully manoeuvring onto a verge by a deep dyke. There's hardly an inch to spare. It would not have gone well if we'd turned the wheel to escape the lorry. We really are lucky to be alive. The CD player tries to jump back to life and he quickly kills it. Now is not the time for any more HAM. I'm shaking and I know it's not just the cold. It's partly shock and it's partly absolute elation that we're still alive. All kinds of chemicals are now shooting round my system.

As we get into a steady speed, much slower than before, Thor turns his head to look at me twice, like he wants to ask something and daren't. On the third go he finally spits it out.

'Tanz, who was that by the stopped car? I couldn't see them, just a shadow. And where the fuck did they go?'

I close my eyes and swallow. I don't really want to say it out loud as it's my special secret. My get-out-of-jail card in a world that's sometimes too lonely and too tedious and too damn domestic.

'He's looking after me. He's one of yours.'

He stares at me for too long. He should be looking at the road.

'*Huldufólk?*'

I nod and he looks back out front again, thank Christ.

'His name is Alfvin. I saw him by the waterfall today too.'

To my surprise, Thor's chest heaves with emotion and he has to breathe for a moment to get himself under control. I stroke his back – no mean feat while he's driving.

'Are you okay?'

He nods. 'Do you know how lucky you are? So many people have stories about meeting one of the Hidden Ones, as children. Hardly anyone is lucky enough to have met one as an adult and know it.'

'You seem very ready to accept my story.'

'Of course I accept it. Someone stopped us from dying tonight, in the nick of time, then totally disappeared.'

'I know. But he didn't disappear, he was still watching. I heard him.'

Thor is silent for a while as he takes this in. 'I was saved from drowning as a child. Brought back to shore. No one knew who saved me, but I did. I said it was a woman who disappeared afterwards, but she wasn't a woman, she was more than a woman. You've made me so happy. You're also more than a woman. You're a magic Geordie.'

Hearing him suddenly say 'Geordie' pulls me out of my emotional state and into the giggles. I can't stop and soon neither can he. We're alive, we were saved. It has to be for a reason. Tonight isn't just a ghost hunt. It's a mission. We have a mission. And right now that feels pretty okay.

VIKING WARRIOR WOMAN

By the time we reach the summer house, the laughter has receded somewhat. It takes quite a while and I'm suddenly starving. We're also both knackered. We park up and enter, glad of the heating being on. They don't have to worry about the expense of bills over here, as 90 per cent of heating comes from water already made hot underground. Thor told me that this afternoon. It's lovely and toasty as we walk in and Thor immediately goes to the fridge and starts preparing supper for us both. I swear, in London, you could hire this man out for hundreds of quid an hour; there's absolutely nothing he doesn't just go ahead and do without being begged. I stand and listen at the door for crying or any sign of why I've been called back so urgently but there's nothing, and within the shortest time we're eating stir-fried tofu with a bunch of vegetables which came out of the freezer, and a beautiful spicy sauce that he threw together out of nowhere. The wine that he pours with it is perfection. A very light red. After we've eaten, we begin to sink into the sofa and I can see Thor's eyes drooping. That is until the banging starts on the windows.

At first I think it's only me who can hear it, as surely Thor would've had this happen before over the years if he was a 'sensitive'? Plus, he doesn't seem to react straight away. But then I notice him staring at me intently with a shocked looked on his face, probably wondering if I can hear what he can hear.

'This is what I told you about, Thor. She's not happy.'

'Okay, so this is terrifying.' He puts his hands over his ears and for the first time since he showed up to save me, I can see he's very ruffled. His eyes show fear; why wouldn't they? This is the unknown. I speak up.

'STOP THAT RACKET AT ONCE. I'll come out, if you stop the dramatics.'

The banging immediately ceases.

'Tanz, did you just tell a ghost to shut up?'

'Yes, I did and I'll do it again if she doesn't pack it in!'

'Do I have to come outside with you?'

'Absolutely not. Stay in here, get the coffee going and await instructions. If you hear something that sounds like me being murdered, only then do you leave your post. I need a sentry. The rest I can handle myself.'

In real life, I'm not sure I can do this by myself, but I have a very strong feeling about my sister-witch who lives down the road and I'm going to go with my gut. I kiss Thor on the cheek and he hugs me.

'You are a Viking warrior woman. You are Freyja. I am in awe.'

'So you should be. Wish me luck. See you soon.'

'Good luck.'

I zip up my gigantic (stolen from the cupboard) coat and venture outside, wondering what the hell the night holds for me. I'm not sure anything could be worse than a lorry almost killing me, though, so I step onto the stoop with as much confidence as possible. And even as I wonder what the hell is going to happen, I'm again caught up in how beautiful this country is. The snow has now mostly melted but instead it's icy, and the mist hangs heavily over the landscape. It's like another planet: romantic and insane, just like me. To my surprise, Thor follows me out. He's carrying two shot glasses.

'Don't worry, Tanz, I know who the witch is here. I just want to clink glasses with you before you begin. Infuse your night with luck.'

I take the shot and knock it back. It tastes medicinal and fucking delicious. I don't know what it is, it's certainly not that ghastly liquorice-y *Brennivín*, but I do feel I've tasted it before, and it warms me to my toes. I smile at Thor and he puts his forehead to mine.

'All magic and love. You'll be fine. You're amazing.'

'Yes, I am. I'll give you a shout if I can't cope.'

He nods, then goes back inside. I like that man, he has class. My body is now toasty from the inside out. That shot was something else. I look towards the bush where I saw the crying woman last time; I see nothing. I have a strong pull towards the rowan tree, though. I need to stand by it, that's the overwhelming feeling that I get, so that's what I do. I wrap my arm around the trunk like it's an old friend and kiss the bark. I don't give a monkey's how crackers I may look at this point. No one's watching and I just want the rowan tree to know that I care. It's almost like I feel a heartbeat from this amazing, protective tree as I lean against the trunk and listen for anything out of place. At first all I hear is the quiet of the night. But then I sense crying from an upset woman which builds. Her sobs are further away than last time, out among the small, bushy spruces, and overlaid by the sobbing of a child from another direction. They don't meld together, they're coming from different places, which is very confusing. I don't know how I can handle this on my own. If Sheila was here, she'd solve this conundrum in a minute. But my confusion is muddying the situation, and it occurs to me that I've got to clear out pointless thoughts. Someone is demanding attention and they obviously didn't die happily. So I calm my brain and breathe slowly and deeply, asking for help from wherever I can get it.

Of course, that is exactly when a battery-powered lantern appears around the side of the cabin and a familiar smoke-tinged voice calls, 'Hallllooooo.'

'Birta!'

'I saw your lights on, all the way from mine. Thought I'd come check if you'd returned.'

She reaches me and gives me a big hug, though some of the effect is lost as we're both in padded coats.

'I had a feeling you'd show up. I put a call out with my witchy sonar. You got my note, I presume?'

'I did. It was fine, I went home and painted more.' She shines the lantern in my face.

'Oi, what are you doing?'

'Just want to see those sparkly eyes in the light. You're such a pretty witch.'

'Ha! So are you.'

She looks up at the windows of the house. Thor is peering out.

'Two questions: who's that in there, and what are you doing out here alone?'

'That's Thor, the real owner of this place. Long story. And I'm out here alone because the crying ghost who's haunting this house asked me to come back, then when I did, she started knocking at all the windows again. She stopped when I told her off, but it made things a bit too real for Thor so I've made him stand guard for me from inside. He'd probably be more hindrance than help at this moment. I just KNEW you'd come. Do you want to go in and have a hot drink or something?'

She shakes her head vehemently.

'No. I don't need a drink, I just want to help you solve the mystery of the sad lady. If she's called you back here and is banging at the windows, she really must have something to tell you.'

'Oh, she's very determined.'

'So how can I help you?'

'I think if we stick together, your energy might help magnify mine. I could hear crying just as you arrived, but from two different directions, and I'm very confused. She's crying and a child is crying. I need to know what the hell happened to these people. Maybe if we walk towards where I heard her first . . .'

'Okay. Perhaps I should hang back while you find her.

She may not recognize me or want another person there. I'll power you from the rear.'

I snigger. I can't help it. Double entendres are my absolute favourite. Birta rolls her eyes. 'Should I switch off the light?'

'Yes please, that's how I saw her last time.'

I advance slowly forwards, away from all illumination from the windows. Without light it feels colder, but I don't care. Not dying tonight in a horrible lorry accident, then hearing the voice of Alfvin, has given me some kind of extra boost in power, or energy, or whatever, and it's surging through me right now. It kicked in when the banging started on the windows again. *Time for action, time to push forward. You can solve this.* I could feel it rather than hear it; Frank's voice has been on mute most of the time since I touched down in Keflavík. It's like he handed my latest spooky education over to someone else, as this isn't his territory.

Birta keeps about ten feet behind me. She's a stealthy lass but I can still hear her thick clothes rubbing together as she moves. Ahead I suddenly hear a voice. Not weeping but sad, talking quietly to herself. I hold my hand up so Birta knows I've found her. Birta stops walking. I come forward another five steps and she materializes on the ground ahead. Her hair is long and dark, her eyes are haunted and she's sitting there, arms around her knees, wrapped in a grubby blanket. I can't tell what the stains are, they may just be mud, but they may also be blood. I sit on the ground and inch forward on my bum, hoping she won't disappear. She doesn't, and I get the feeling she's going nowhere. She watches me without once shifting her gaze, intently examining my face. When she speaks she sounds like she did in my head earlier. Far away, like she's coming at me through a dream or dense fog, but precise and determined.

'*You see me.*'

'Yes, I see you. What's your name?'

'*Helene. I'm Helene.*'

'Hello, Helene.'

'*No one ever saw me. You see me.*'

'I'm here to help.'

'*Yes. Help.*'

'Do you know what happened to you?'

'*I've lost Paul. He's not with me.*'

'Paul. Is that your husband?'

Tears begin to stream down her face, making rivulets through dirt which I assume is soil. I had a dream recently of clods of earth hitting me as I lay in a hole. In a hole but still alive. Alive for ever. Now I get it. It's now clear this lady is not Icelandic, which is quite the revelation. There's no trace of an accent in her voice, she's a softly spoken English woman.

'Where are you from?'

She thinks. '*Surrey. Parents from Surrey. Paul?*'

'Yes, is Paul a child?'

'*My son. You know him?*'

'No, but . . . I heard a child crying . . .'

'*Yes, he's all alone, I think. I can't see him. Where is he?*'

'I'll find out for you. I'll do my best. Do you remember what happened?'

'*I was in the bedroom. A gun went off. Nobody knows.*

Nobody knows the secret. But you see me. Paul's only three, he'll be frightened. I have to find him.'

I get an overwhelming feeling just then that I have to touch Helene. I'm not even sure she's made of anything solid. But something makes me inch forwards again, take off the glove that I nicked from the drawer upstairs, and reach out my hand. To my surprise, she does the same and her freezing cold fingertips meet mine, solid as anything. I take hold of her hand, hoping to warm it, but I think I know even as I do so that it will remain as cold as frozen cement. She smiles at me and she has such a warm face when she smiles. A face filled with compassion, pain and kindness. As I look into her eyes, I suddenly see snippets of her life, like a show-reel, inside my head.

She came here for a new start with her husband. Something had gone wrong and she didn't want to lose him. The place where they lived didn't look like the cabin I'm in now. But it wasn't far away. I calm my thoughts so I can make room for more information. And there 'he' is, his pixelated face, hard to fix on how he looked. Definitely bearded, the one I saw making love to her so dispassionately in my vision, the one I'm convinced I saw standing on the cliff edge when I first laid eyes on Alfvin, in my London dreams.

I'm shown that Helene was a good cook, could sew, worked hard with the few animals they had. 'He' would go off and do work for people in exchange for provisions. They were doing some kind of off-grid thing like Birta, but without frills or nice coffee makers. Everything was hard wrought, but she toughed it out while also making life as much fun as possible for her son. She was the unassuming backbone of their little gang of three and she kept this pipe dream of her husband's going, though deep inside she knew it was hard and barren and difficult to maintain. When I put the feelers out, I sense that this wasn't a permanent arrangement, it was a time-controlled event, like 'time out' for a year or something. But whatever messed with their marriage before began to creep in again. She felt it and she finally started to acknowledge that her husband wasn't going to change. Helene knew something wasn't right when 'he' became more distant, cruel with his words and didn't want to have sex with her. When he did, it was without feeling or tenderness. One day she took a risk when her son was napping, and went to check what her husband was up to. She saw him having sex with someone else. Helene didn't even know he was doing odd jobs for a woman; she thought the work was for a man. But there he was having a wonderful time in someone else's arms, experiencing a sensuality she could only dream of, and she ran off screaming, half mad with grief.

I'm so sad for her when I see this, but I'm also very scared. That man was cold and full of secrets and I can already sense what happened when the wife he was tired of followed him and discovered what he'd been up to. I can't 'see' what happened after she got home and locked herself in the bedroom. But I know he shot her, and I suspect he did the same to his son. This poor woman who only came here for her husband's sake was murdered and probably disposed of. Which is why she's wandering around the Icelandic countryside looking for Paul.

'How do I find you, Helene? And Paul? How?'

She opens her mouth to speak then suddenly I hear an angry bellow, like a rutting bull, and the ground vibrates. Immediately Helene disappears, her hand pulling from my grasp. One second there, the next gone. I have no idea what just happened.

I look around me. Nothing. I stand and I hear Birta saying my name in a stage whisper. I'm impressed: loud whispering is an art form.

'It's okay, you can come out, she's gone.'

A light goes on behind a bush, then Birta stands, flexing her knees a couple of times.

'What happened, Tanz? I couldn't see her, just you talking to someone, then sitting there with your hand out like you were in a trance. Here, I have my flask. Let's sit and have a moss tea.'

So I perch on a rock big enough for two, as close to Birta as possible for warmth, and we sip our teas out of tin cups as I explain everything that Helene showed me.

'He was having an affair. But I don't know why he had to shoot his wife and child when he was found out.'

Birta shivers. She looks really quite devastated. 'What a horrible story.'

It's when she says this that I'm reminded how much less mortified I am than others, these days, when I find out about grisly premature deaths. Her reaction is the right one. I mean, Iceland isn't exactly brimming with murders anyway, so it's obviously going to strike at Birta's heart to hear of such horrors. But it's interesting to note that I seem to be much more matter of fact in the face of grim death nowadays, after encountering so much of it since I became friends with Sheila. I'm not sure it's good that I'm so desensitized, though maybe if I wasn't, I'd have a nervous breakdown, and be no good to the spooks any more.

'Sorry, Birta, I've come across so much of this in the past eighteen months that I expect there to be evil deeds here, there and everywhere.'

'It must have been very hard for you.'

'It's been emotional as much as anything else. I've encountered bad women as well as bad men in this world and the spirit world, but all of the murderers I've "met" so far, alive and dead, have been men, and fuck me, they were all brutal. This is just another one.'

'For a man to bring his wife so many miles from home, along with his child, then abuse that privilege so flagrantly and pull out a gun when he gets found out? What kind of savage would do that?'

'One who thinks they're the centre of the universe and everyone else is a bit player in the film of their life.'

She nods at me. 'Nicely put.'

'What I don't understand is how he got away with it. She said something about a secret? It can't have been that long ago. The way she looked and dressed it won't be more than forty years ago. Is there any murder you know of where a bloke shot his English wife and son?'

'Are you kidding me? If that was a known murder, there would be about twenty books written about it. We're all readers and writers here. Plus, it would have been such a big story, it would be in folklore, talked about all the time.'

'Well, that's just crazy. I have to say, apart from the beard and the cold and secretive nature, she really didn't let me see much of him. Like he's protected or unreachable. Why is that? I mean, *what if he's still alive*? He could be in Iceland, living out his self-obsessed old age, chewing on fetid shark whenever he feels like it, as if nothing happened!'

Birta chuckles and downs the last of her tea.

'How do you make even the most disgusting and awful circumstances comical? That's quite a skill you have, you maniac.'

'That's me. Inappropriate Geordie loon.'

'Anyway I, for one, don't think the bearded murderer is still around. Do you feel he's alive?'

'No, I don't. I just hope he's not messing with poor Helene because that angry noise right before she disappeared could easily have been an enraged man. I met a ghost before who was controlling and terrorizing a little boy that he'd killed, even though they'd both been dead for over a hundred years.'

'Oh my goodness. What happened?'

'I set the little boy free, reunited him with his mum, and then gave the bully what for. He's gone, never to return.'

Birta pours the last of the flask of tea into both our mugs and looks meaningfully at me. The energy between us is that of two old witches who've known each other for four hundred years. I don't know a lot about past lives but if they're real, then I've known Birta before for definite.

'Tanz, did it occur to you that you've ended up here with this job to do, this mission, because you have experience in the field? You've handled a situation not unlike this before, so you were pulled here to help another soul who couldn't move on?'

'It doesn't sound like an impossibility when you put it like that, but Sheila, my good friend, has a lot more experience than I have in the whole spiritual realm and I'm sure many others do too. Any one of them could have come in and helped Helene.'

'Oh, really? So Sheila and others would have the vivaciousness and courage to jump on a plane to Iceland, virtually on a whim, within a day or two of thinking of it? Sheila and others would already have experience of falling for self-centred bastards with sexual charm, therefore understanding why this woman ended up in the torment she's in now? Sheila and these others would mentally be happy after being snowed in and terrified by a banging ghost to return the next day and help her because they "felt" she needed it? That's a lot of factors, Tanz, and you fit the bill. The perfect choice.'

'I would never have thought of it like that, but it's actually pretty incredible to think that the law of attraction brought me all the way to Iceland to help someone I have no connection with.'

'You don't know there's no connection. Things unfold in their own time. There may well be a connection and you've just not seen it yet.'

'Okay, well, that makes the past week seem a little less randomly hardcore. It also explains some of the ridiculous "coincidences" that have gone on. Meeting Einar after a fun ghost-bust in Hampstead, meeting Thor after I landed here, and getting his number, then finding out he knows Einar and owns the place where I got snowed in. Meeting you with your quiet magic, backing me up when I'm chatting to spooks. The whole thing has felt guided, I can't deny it.'

'You know, I don't think you've reached anywhere near your full power or potential in life yet, Tanz. The best is yet to come. The less you worry about how you look, what you say, what other people think of your witchy ways, and what stupid men think of you, the more formidable you're going to get. Just "be", Tanz. I feel honoured to have met someone like you, you're genuinely unique. And I hate people so you're quite honoured too.'

I kiss her cheek then shiver from within my giant coat.

'Thank you, my beautiful new friend. I'd love to carry on this conversation but not while developing frostbite in my extremities. Why don't you come in for a drink?'

'You already know I'm going to say no, don't you?! I have an idea for a painting and I'm itching to do it now, with a bunch of gas lamps and candles for light. You have company tonight so I don't feel so bad. I have my cats and a bottle of very nice wine. That's all the company I need.'

'You are a fucking legend, Birta. Thank you so much for being my back-up team just now.'

'And you swear like a sailor, Tanz. It's funny.'

'You about tomorrow evening? I have an idea.'

'Okay. I'll keep a watch for the porch light going on tomorrow evening. If it does, I'll know you want me to visit.'

'Perfect. Though it would be easier if you just got a phone.'

She stands and puts her little backpack on, ready to walk home.

'Not as much fun, though. This feels like espionage.'

1976

Thor has the face of a nervous child when I come back through the door. I smile at him and his body relaxes as I pull off the giant duvet of a coat that I appropriated from the cupboard.

We sit by the wood burner with wine in hand as I give him the basics of what happened. He is suitably impressed and goes into 'helpful' mode when I tell him I'll need his services tomorrow too. Says he's very happy to drive me wherever I need to go. He also puts on some music and I laugh when it turns out to be the Abba album I was listening to the other night.

'I wouldn't imagine you as an Abba man, Thor.'

'I'm not. Someone must have left the album here, it's not mine. I don't even know why I put it on.'

I decide to get up and have a little boogie to 'Dancing Queen'. Thor gives me a round of applause, but remains curled up and comfy on the sofa. Just as I do a twirl, I see Helene in my head, making bread in the same kitchen I envisaged before, 'Dancing Queen' leaking out of a tiny radio. She's swaying as she kneads the dough. I feel this wasn't long before she died, and I also feel like this song was brand new then.

'What year did this song come out, Thor, do you know?'

He looks at the album cover, and eventually exclaims '1976! That's when the album came out. And this was the big single, wasn't it?'

'Indeed it was. My little mam loves Abba and she *loves* "Dancing Queen".'

'I think most mums loved Abba!'

He's doing his best to stay chipper, but Thor's eyes are drooping.

'Should we get some sleep, Thor? It's been quite the day.'

'I'm sorry, Tanz, I'm a lightweight.'

'No you're not, you've done a lot today. Plus, we nearly died, but didn't. It's all a lot to take in. I'm absolutely bushed.'

'You can have the big bed as that's where you were already sleeping, I'll take the smaller room. Unless you'd like me to hold you until you fall asleep?'

Much as a warm embrace would be welcome, I'm pretty sure it wouldn't remain just that, and there really has been enough sex flying about the place since I met Einar. I shake my head and laugh.

'Naughty Thor!'

'You can't blame a man for trying. And I mean it anyway, I would happily just keep you warm if that's what you wanted. I'm not a beast.'

Not for one second do I feel threatened or uncomfortable in this man's company. His word is his bond, I can tell.

So I cuddle him like a best friend to say goodnight, then go and fall into bed. Today has been so twisty-turny and last night my sleep was nowhere near as long or as deep as it could have been. I have some catching up to do.

THE LAUGHING ELF

I wake up in the pitch black. The room is preternaturally inky, but this is no dream. There is someone else here; I can't hear breathing or movement, I just feel the closeness of 'another'. I look to the bottom of the bed and in the deeper-than-it-should-be darkness I can make out someone sitting on the wooden ottoman. They are made of shadow, hard to define, but definitely there. Tall and quiet and still. I wonder if I should be scared, but deep down I know that I'm not. I'm too in awe. I roll the small bell at my neck between my forefinger and thumb, so it makes the tiniest tinkling sound, then hold my breath so I can listen harder. I don't know if I should speak. As I stare into the gloom I can see the glow of starlight in his pupils. That's how I know he's looking straight at me.

I whisper, 'Alfvin?'

'*Yes.*'

His voice reminds me of the voice that comes to me from my deepest recesses. The one that Frank won't explain to me. The wisest and most unfathomable. His has a touch more resonance, but they feel like they're made of the same stuff. Calm and not to be argued with.

'Thank you for stopping us tonight. We would have died without your help.'

'*Protecting you. You are important. Chosen.*'

'Chosen for what?'

'*You are going to right a wrong. You understand, you are open to* goðsögn. *To myth. And I will lead you to a sacred place, a place of bones. You must make sure that when others come, they don't trample* Huldufólk *land. I will show you where the bones are, and that must be the end of it, no searching anywhere else. We folk of myth don't like to be disturbed. We have guarded the bones, they must be surrendered, but we are private ones. I will show you exactly where. After you uncover the truth of the bones, you will be signposted. I must protect our land. We will not have disturbance.*'

'Okay. But what if I can't find out the truth? I saw Helene's ghost tonight, but she can't tell me directly. I thought I should ask someone in town tomorrow then come back, but what if no one knows anything?'

Alfvin makes a sound and for a moment I don't know what it is, then it hits me. That gruff little 'cough, cough' noise was a laugh. He just laughed. I see the glow of his eyes intensify, the Hidden-Folk version of a humorous twinkle. '*You are not in this alone. Have you not found every answer with ease so far? Have you not been guided? How could you not find the truth? You will see.*'

'Okay, so you're not wrong, it's been insane. And you . . .'

'Yes.'

'You've restored my faith.'

'Good. You think too much of human things. They are not for you. Tomorrow, secrets will unlock. Truths will reveal themselves. You will set a trapped soul free. Right now, close your eyes and lie back. I will show you.'

I do as I'm told. All at once I feel the lightest of touches on my arm. I want to open my eyes and look at him properly, but I can't. My eyelids are welded together and *whoosh*, I'm out of my body and, like I dreamed before, straddling a giant eagle. Now it's daylight and I'm swooping over and around Mount Esja. I know it's her because I can feel her energy. There is powdery snow atop her and there are rivulets of white ice in her cracks and folds. Behind me I feel the light touch at my waist of another. I can't look round, I can't reach back, but I know it's Alfvin. He speaks calmly in my ear as I feel the euphoria of absolute freedom.

'You will not fall. You will not plummet. You will not lose the power to fly. But when you give your power to others, you hover lower to the ground and sometimes you land and can't take off again, for too much time. Does this make you happy?'

'No. Of course not.'

'And yet you, Northern Witch, Finder of Truths, Vessel of Love, hand over your ability to swoop and ride the air to those who want to take from you and not give back. This is an insecure human thing. It kills spirit, it steals the life force. No other human should complete you. No other should shore up your earth-made pain. Only you can do that, you

are your magic. And you make your own sex magic. A companion should complement what you already are. What you already have. Then you will always fly.'

Okay, so when I was told that Icelanders believed in elves, this is definitely not what I envisaged. This wise, level-voiced being just summed up how and why I fuck up my life. Also, I really like the sound of 'sex magic'. The eagle begins to climb, until we're riding a thermal way above the land. Esja is far below, the power of the 'female' pounding through her lava-formed veins. The sea is singing all around her. We glide at this height and Alfvin leans into my ear again and I have to strain to hear his next words.

'*Lessons will not be easy, Chosen. But you can take them. No matter how much it feels that you can't, you will be able to take whatever comes, and magic will be your cushion. It will hurt but you will always land safely, then fly again. Trust.*'

Now the eagle swoops at an alarming rate, taking us into a dive towards the sea, like the dream I had before. But this time, I am not plummeted to a watery grave, because within about ten feet of the water surface, this feathered genius deftly swoops back up again, shooting us towards the clouds. It's the most exciting, energizing feeling you could ever have. And just as I'm about to whoop with joy I hear '*Protected*' whispered in my ear and I jolt awake in the dark of the bedroom. There's the teeniest tinkle of a bell, I'm not sure if it's the one at my neck or not as I'm disorientated, but I sense immediately that Alfvin has gone. And the loneliness of this absence hits me like a Frisbee in the solar plexus and I burst into big, fat sobs. Before I can stifle them, Thor, hair all akimbo and, like me, still mostly dressed, stumbles into the room.

'Are you okay, Tanz?'

Through my sobs I explain as best I can. 'I'm so sorry, Thor, I had . . . a dream . . . It was beautiful and I got a . . . a shock . . . when I woke up . . . So sorry . . .'

He climbs onto the bed and scoots up so he's spooning me, then wraps his arms around me.

'Don't worry, I'm here.'

My tears subside quickly as I settle into his embrace. There is so much to be unpicked from what Alfvin just revealed to me. Having these things explained is one thing. Actually changing my life so I don't keep making the same mistakes, pulling down my own power to fit in with other people, men for the most part, is quite another. Habits are not easy to break, especially not life-long, deep-rooted, self-defeating ones. Luckily, I can feel myself sinking into snoozy relaxation with Thor's arms keeping me warm and his breaths turning into tiny, almost imperceptible snores. I swear he snores like a cat; it's very sweet. I decide to let go of self-reflection for now, and just enjoy sleeping up close to a beautiful man with a fabulous chest-rug who isn't going to run off to a casino.

It's the little things.

ERNEST LAMB

I wake up to the sky beginning to get light at 10 a.m. and a tray being placed down on the bed next to me. I can't believe how long I slept, uninterrupted. Thor has made door-step-sized wedges of toast, with butter and chunky strawberry jam on the side, plus great big mugs of coffee. It smells as delicious as anything I've been brought in my life, but also makes me feel emotional as it's been done out of pure loveliness.

'Thor, will you be my servant for ever, please?'

'Of course.'

My worry here is I think he means it. But it's not a major concern. I'm very flattered, truth be told. I butter us both a wedge each then we share the spoon as we measure out how much jam we each want. We then sit up in bed, eating our breakfasts, and Thor describes a dream he had.

'I saw a cave, Tanz. It had an opening of rocks, covered in thick moss, and music was coming out of there. But not normal music, primal stuff, drumming that buried itself in the bottom of my belly.'

'I've been feeling that since I arrived here. That drumming in the pit of my stomach.'

'You're kidding?'

'I think you know by now that I don't kid about any of this stuff. I am literally as crazy as I sound.'

He looks at me very seriously, then stares down at his coffee like he's afraid.

'I hope I didn't make you uncomfortable by coming to your bed last night.'

'Actually, no. I didn't realize how much I needed comfort. The Einar thing really had messed with me, plus the past few days have been extremely discombobulating.'

'Extremely what?'

'Sorry. Confusing, discomfiting. I came flying out here to spend time with a man who didn't care. Then I was stuck here and forced to see that my actual purpose wasn't to do with Einar, it was about helping a trapped spirit. And then you and I nearly got killed, then I spoke to a ghost last night, and had a really meaningful dream that made me cry. That's a bloody lot, isn't it?'

'Indeed.'

'So of course, a hug was what I needed more than anything. I just couldn't see it, 'til you showed up and forced it on me. In the nicest way possible. Then I slept SO HARD!'

Thor smiles at me. 'Good to know . . .'

He doesn't get any further as suddenly there's a knocking from downstairs. So far, any banging I've heard here has come from a determined ghost. But this sounds like someone with actual hands, in the actual real world, rapping the door knocker with a fair bit of purpose. I jump up and put on a grey fleecy robe I found on the first night here.

'I think we might be about to get some answers, Thor, I feel it.'

'Wait for me!'

Thor climbs out of bed and grabs something off the floor . . . A huge cream woollen sweater that he must have shrugged off in the night. As he puts it on, he lets me know, 'You're not going down there on your own.'

We descend together, like curious explorers, and I only jump a teensy bit when the knocker raps again. This is definitely not a haunting, more like an impatient, lost person. Or Birta.

When I open the door, there's no Birta and no ghost. It's a smallish older bloke in a suit, with unruly sandy hair, a bald bit in the middle, a softly drooping chin and big glasses over alert, milky blue eyes. He gives a sort of bow and announces himself.

'Hello, I'm Ernest Lamb.'

His voice is nasal and more than a bit Essex. Completely bloody unexpected in the circumstances. He really isn't in a warm enough coat for this weather, and once or twice he looks to the car he arrived in, like he wants to be back in it, cocooned in the warmth of the heaters.

'Hello, Ernest. What can I do for you?'

'Well, could I be an absolute imposition and come in out of the cold first?'

I'm not a fan of letting just anyone into the place but the poor fella's nose is turning blue. Thor nods at the stranger. 'This is my friend Tanz and I'm Thor. Come in.'

He's so polite and proper, bless him. Ernest steps gratefully through into the heated living room and I offer him a coffee after closing the door.

'Very civilized, but I don't suppose you have tea?'

Just like my parents then. Cup of English breakfast tea or nothing. Thor laughs.

'One of my friends brought me a box from London as a gift. It's in the kitchen. I only have UHT milk, I'm afraid.'

Ernest rubs his hands together. 'That's fine. Leave the bag in and just a splash of milk. I like my spoon standing up.'

Okay, so he's a character. Still doesn't explain him driving around the freezing countryside before the sun's even properly risen. Without his coat he's in a grey shirt with a maroon tie with a stain on it. I start lighting up the wood burner and motion to Ernest to sit on the sofa, which he happily does.

'So, Ernest, are you lost?'

'Not exactly. I'm, errr . . . here on behalf of someone else . . . In Iceland, I mean. I've promised to find as many answers as I can for a nice lady called Carol Coleman. I'm a private investigator.'

He looks quite proud as he says it and, to be honest, I'm impressed. Nobody loves *Magnum, P.I.* more than I do.

'Oh, wow, are you? That's cool, isn't it, Thor?'

Thor approaches us with a tray. There's a huge mug of tea for Ernest, more coffee for us and a plate with the second packet of those killer little pink-topped cakes arranged on it. Fucking hell, bang goes the diet again. Those fancies are like crack. I'm eyeing them up before he even puts the tray down.

'Tanz seems to find herself in the most interesting situations. Now we have a private investigator over for breakfast. I love it. Who or what are you looking for exactly?'

'Oh, it's a woman. Carol's aunt. She came over here in the seventies then never contacted the family again, apart from one letter sent at the end of 1976. She was called Helene.'

My mouth opens and I have to close it again. Alfvin doesn't mess around when he says there'll be 'guidance' and I'll find the truth. Looks like a bunch of answers just rapped on the door and demanded a cuppa. Thor doesn't say anything, though I see an eyebrow rise and a twinkle in his eye. He loves all of this stuff, obviously. Ernest takes a good slug of his tea then nods appreciatively.

'Not a terrible cuppa.'

This amuses Thor, who takes a tiny bow. 'Why thank you.'

'So, Ernest, what did you hope to find when you drove out here today? Are we allowed to know the story? This place belongs to Thor's family; I'm just a friend but maybe we can help.' I'm all ears but I don't want to tell Ernest anything until I'm sure. I like to delay the moment when people decide I'm crackers.

'Actually, it's no secret so I can give you a rundown. Maybe, Thor, your family will know something that can help?'

Ernest takes a cake, inspects it, then bites. His eyes light up at the flavour. Another fan. I'll have to nick a second one before he gets into a feeding frenzy. They're *that* good.

'So Carol, my client, her mum died a few years ago and there was a box of stuff she didn't look at when she cleared her mum's house, she just put it in storage and forgot about it. But recently she went there to get something and on a whim started looking through the box. Her mother had always said that she drove her sister away and didn't talk about it much, but when Carol found a picture of Helene, plus letters, then the supposed "final" one, she smelled a rat. The family didn't talk about Helene because they were so upset. Apparently she married a man who was absolute trouble. He had an affair and left her with their toddler son, completely devastated her, then he came back and she welcomed him with open arms. Completely infatuated apparently. Carol's mum begged her not to get back with him, then they had a blazing row when Helene said she was off on an adventure to live in a remote farm building in Iceland with him. Apparently it was to rebuild their marriage "away from the world", but Carol's mum thought he was probably running from some trouble he'd caused. The day before Helene flew away with him and the son, Carol asked her to reconsider, pleaded, and there was another huge row. And that was the last she saw or heard of her sister and nephew apart from one, extremely strange letter.'

'Woah. Strange how?' I'm completely dazzled. I just know this is who I've been seeing. Poor Helene, blinded by love, or lust, or whatever it is that makes us get obsessed with people that are terrible for us.

'Well, they corresponded over the years, Helene and Carol's mum Jocelyn. Helene was a bit of a hippy adventurer before she met the husband, and would go travelling for a month or two at a time. She'd write letters, and there was a very definite way that she phrased things. She also had extremely distinctive curvy handwriting. Before this man came along, the sisters were very cordial. Anyway, the last letter, after Helene went off to Iceland, came eight months later, posted from Dublin. It was typewritten and just said she was living in Ireland with her husband and son, and that she wanted nothing more to do with the family that rejected her "belovid" husband. Spelled like that b-e-l-o-v-i-d. Now Carol believes her mother considered it a mistake, born out of anger or upset, but not once in any of her correspondence did Helene spell a single word wrong. She was very clever. Also, it was suspicious that she would type the letter, when every single other time she wrote on lined paper with a blue pen. And to top it all off, she signed it in that distinctive handwriting but there were two places where the lines looked "doubled", like someone had signed then gone over it again to make sure it looked right. Which actually just made it look to me, and to Carol, very, very wrong.'

He nods at me meaningfully, takes a slow slurp of tea and grabs another cake. That was quite a lot of talking so he deserves it, I guess.

Thor sips his coffee thoughtfully then pipes up. 'Ernest, do you think they lived in this house? Is that why you knocked?'

'No, not this house exactly, but my research suggests this place was built over the foundations of a dilapidated farm building that they did stay in. It was in such a mess it was razed by the builder at the end of the seventies and this was built over it.'

I glance at Thor now, unable to contain my excitement. 'Oh, that explains it.'

Now Ernest looks confused. 'Explains what?'

'Are you ready to hear something weird?'

Ernest nods, not looking that ready at all, just a bit bamboozled.

'So the lady you're investigating, Helene, you've seen a photo of her?'

'I have.'

'Long brown hair, delicate features, big brown eyes, lovely face when she smiles, slightly lost expression when she doesn't?'

Now I've piqued his interest, his tone is eager. 'Indeed. How do you know? Did you find some photos?'

'No, I did not. I also know that she had a soft, well-spoken voice, was born in Surrey, her son was called Paul, that they came here on some kind of short-term let to experience an Icelandic "adventure" for a period of months, maybe a year. When they got here it wasn't what she thought it would be at all. The place was a damp, cold dump and her husband was inattentive to their son and grew colder and colder towards her. Especially so when he started doing "jobs" for a neighbour. Helene thought it was a male neighbour but it wasn't, it was a woman. Whatever affair he'd had before, she'd hoped he'd changed his ways but he hadn't. One day she spied on them having sex and it drove her so mad she ran away screaming. Because of that he knew he was discovered, and he wasn't happy about it. I don't know anything about who he had the affair with or what the complete timeline is but for some reason, being discovered like that sent him into such a rage that he killed his family. From everything else I can gather he then fucked off, because how else would a letter be posted from Dublin, unless maybe he had an accomplice?'

Ernest's jaw is about two inches off the floor.

'How . . . ? What am I missing here?'

Thor smiles proudly. 'Tanz sees ghosts and Helene's is here. And she's not in a very good mood. Always banging at the windows. She told Tanz a lot of things.'

I can see from Ernest's demeanour that he's not having this in the slightest and would probably like to go back to his car right this instant.

'No offence, you two, but this isn't really my territory. I deal in facts.' He regards me, completely deadpan, looking for traces of a joke or a lie. 'Are you pulling my leg?'

'No, I'm not. This isn't the first time this has happened to me. I've accidentally "solved" several cases due to spooks insisting on telling me their stories and at some point *every time* this has happened: at least one person has looked at me the way you are now. Including a policeman in St Albans who had to rescue me from a creepy murderer called Dan, whose dead wife wasn't pleased with him in the slightest.'

Something changes in Ernest's eyes as a thought hits him. 'Wait a minute, are you the one that found that woman in Bluebell Wood? Her husband was the slasher?'

'Yes, but I'd rather not talk about it, thank you. It still triggers the fuck out of me. And it wasn't just me, my mate Sheila was there.'

'I read about that! It sounded far-fetched but whichever

way you looked at it, it was hard to fathom how else you worked it out.'

'We worked it out exactly how we said we worked it out. It was awful and he would've killed the pair of us if his dead wife Mona hadn't stepped in. Plus, the press were a bunch of jackals. Anything else I've done since has been "under the radar". And it always comes to me, not the other way round. I don't do this for fun.'

That's not exactly true, I absolutely love helping people whether they're alive or dead, plus solving mysteries puts me on quite a high. But in my case that high often comes with me nearly being murdered in cold blood. So there is that. Thor is staring at me, shaking his head.

'I didn't know you were nearly killed.'

'Oh yes, more than once.'

Ernest is looking confused again. 'You're friends and you never told him?'

'Well, truth be told, we've only been friends for a matter of hours, really.'

'You what?'

'Another time, Ernest. Let's just say I make friends quickly. In the meantime, I have to find Helene's body and I think I know how. But if I explained it to you right now, you would almost definitely try to get me put away.'

Ernest sits back on the sofa and sighs, shaking his head.

'Thor, do you think you could be a good lad and make me another cuppa? I've got to drive back to my hotel soon and report to Carol and, to be honest, I don't know where to start with this. Another nice cup of cha should help put my head straight.'

Thor dutifully jumps up to put the kettle on and then Ernest looks at me, his pate getting a bit shiny as the wood burner adds enough heat to make him perspire.

'Tanz, I don't think you're lying. I also don't bloody know what to make of all this. I'll take a picture of this place from outside if that's okay, plus some of the surroundings so Carol can see the landscape where her aunt and cousin were staying. Whether I tell her everything you told me? . . . It might be better to wait, it would be a lot easier to explain if there were . . . remains.'

'It's up to you what you tell Carol. But I will ask two things. One, do you know what happened to the husband? And two, if I find anything, bones, bodies, whatever, will you please take the "glory"? Tell the press you found them?'

'Now why would you want me to steal your thunder?'

'Because that thunder comes with a lot of unwanted lightning. I don't want to be all over the papers for talking to ghosts. I'd then have to put up with every lunatic in the country trying to contact me, following me around and asking for bloody seances and readings.'

He thinks, then nods decisively.

'So in answer to your first question, the husband changed his name when he came back from Iceland; it took quite a lot of effort to trace him because of that. Lewis Stevens was his final name. He was Jack Thomas when he was with Helene. Turns out he ended up living in a remote part of Ireland where he was eventually killed in a bar fight. The man just couldn't stay out of trouble.'

I feel a shot of relief. That's one thing tied up.

'As for the second, I'm happy to take the credit for anything that'll bolster business for me. But I think I should help you in any way I can or it's false reporting. Here's my card.'

'Thank you, Ernest. You have no idea how much you've helped. I would never have been able to work any of that stuff out on my own, especially in the timeframe. I should've flown home today. I've wasted the fare, and I need to go soon.'

'It's my pleasure.' He regards me intently over his specs. 'Tanz, how do you propose to find the remains? What's the plan?'

There is *no* way I'm telling him this bit. 'I have a gut instinct. Part of my spookiness. It'll be your job to work out a scenario to justify whatever I find.'

His face says he doesn't believe a word of it. I'm pretty sure nobody gets one past Ernest Lamb.

'What a mysterious woman you are, Tanz.'

'Mysterious, or maybe just haunted. Here, let me write down my number in case you come up with anything else pertinent to this.'

'Thank you. By the way, one more thing, Tanz. Jack Thomas, he threatened another of his many women with an axe. He was a violent man. He was indeed running from the law.'

This makes me very sad. 'Of course he was.'

AN OFFERING IN THE FOG

Thor and I have gone outside onto the porch. After Ernest left, we both had enough coffee to sink a battleship, so we've got herbal teas. We're wrapped in coats and blankets and I'm trying to work out what to do next. I need Alfvin to take me to Helene's body but how do I get him to do it? What's his timing? Will he come later?

'Tanz, we need to leave him an offering. Where would be the best place?'

'I didn't think of that. Of course. What are you supposed to leave as an offering to the *Huldufólk*?'

'Traditionally it's food but if you have something else you'd rather leave . . . ? Or we could do both?'

I have a think. The mournful, piping cries of the birds make this landscape even more different from home than it already looks, and the distant hills are disappearing as another mist descends. I can almost see it rolling towards us and can imagine another pea-souper is going to engulf us soon. I'm completely in love with Iceland now, though in the strangest way it was already in my gut. As soon as

I landed it felt like I was attached to the place. I look at the rowan tree. It's so unsurprising that a tree for witchy protection would be right here. And it hits me: obviously that's where the offering should be left, like the bell that hangs round my neck and which I'll treasure for ever. And of course, I know *what* I should leave. A direct swap. The heavy silver and amethyst pendant that I was wearing when I landed. It's something I've treasured and I would give willingly to my wonderful new guide.

'I know what to leave, a precious thing that I'll hang in the rowan. And you can leave a meal at the base of the trunk too. What do you think?'

Thor grins at me. 'You're a true Viking wise woman, Tanz. That's perfect.'

We get to work. Thor goes to the fridge and produces steak, which he brought with him apparently.

'I was going to put it in the freezer for next time guests were here, but I'd rather prepare it for the *Huldufólk*. What an honour!'

He starts to cook and prepare a sauce, while I find my pendant, which I've wrapped up and put in a little zip pocket in my bag. I take it out then wash it under the tap. Knowing a little about silver, I'm well versed in taking off tarnish. I rub the metal with toothpaste, then rinse and polish it up with a towel. It looks gratifyingly clean afterwards, though still like heavy, old silver which is exactly how it should look; I couldn't imagine an ancient, special creature like Alfvin wearing or carrying a shop-bought-looking, over-shiny piece of jewellery. The amethyst is large and oval and a deeper purple than most, going paler near the top. It feels like the right thing to offer, but I need something to hang it from.

Back downstairs, the savoury aromas coming from the kitchen are impressive. Along with everything else, Thor really is a good cook. He points me to a 'craft drawer' in the living room, beneath the TV. There's a sewing kit, buttons, beads and a spool of black nylon cord.

'Bloody hell, Thor, this is perfect! What's it doing here?'

'Oh, I make bracelets sometimes, out of pottery beads and black cord. It's very relaxing.'

'Fucking hell, lad, is there anything you don't do?'

He laughs and shrugs.

'I'm a man of many talents. Here, if you cut it long, I can knot it at each end so that it can be a long or short necklace.'

He does some clever stuff with his hands and suddenly my pendant is on a strong black cord which looks great against the silver. Thor holds the amethyst in his hand and nods.

'This is stunning, Tanz. It feels magical in my palm.'

On impulse I pull down the jumper at my neck and show him the bell.

'I will show very few people this, Thor. My amethyst is in exchange for this gift.'

Thor looks at the bell and his eyes widen as he takes in what I just said. 'I cannot tell you how jealous I am right now, Tanz. That is beyond special.'

Then his eyes glisten with tears and I realize just how much his childhood experience of nearly drowning affected him and how much he reveres the Hidden One who saved him. I put my bell away again and give him a hug.

'You are an amazing human, Thor. Your kindness shines out like a stunning Reykjavík beacon. And your openness is the only way to experience magic. You probably don't even know how magic you are.'

He stands, wiping his eyes. 'I need to take the sauce off the heat.'

Bless him.

When the plate of restaurant-quality-looking food is ready (that lad really is an exceptional cook), we go to the tree outside and Thor places it at the foot of the rowan. Then I find what I think is exactly the same branch that my bell was hanging from, and I drape the pendant. I take Thor's hand, nod to him, then we both bow our heads.

'For Alfvin and the rest of the Hidden Ones. Thank you for your help and guidance. Thank you for saving us from death. Thank you for choosing us. Thank you for my gift. Thank you for restoring my faith. Take these offerings with love, and please, show us what to do next. It's time to take away Helene's suffering.'

Thor then speaks softly in Icelandic and not for the first time I wish I could understand that gorgeous Nordic language. It's the coolest damn thing I ever heard. When he's finished we both nod our heads deeply again and stand quietly. The fog really is rolling in now and I wonder what will happen next. I mean, we can't just stay here and watch, waiting for the offering to be accepted. We have to bugger off and leave it be. We decide to sit at the top of the stoop, farthest away from the tree. It's bloody freezing but so deliciously crisp.

'What do we do now, Thor?'

'If it wasn't for this fog coming in, I'd say let's go and find your friend Birta. I know you say she doesn't like people but I want to meet her. People hide because they've been hurt. It would be nice to greet a neighbour I didn't know about.'

I give him the look that I reckon Ernest Lamb gave me when I said I 'didn't know' how I'd locate Helene's remains.

'You're talking shit, Thor. I've known you five minutes and I can already tell when you're lying.'

He laughs and sticks out his tongue.

'All right, busted. I don't believe in coincidences any more than you do. Everyone you've met in Iceland so far has been another breadcrumb in a trail. I have never met this Birta, she has never walked over to see me when the weather was bad, and she refused to come in and say hello last night, but she certainly came to find *you*. And from what you told me, where she lives may be ramshackle but she's established in there. Either she's been there a long time and completely in hiding, or someone she is close to owned that place before her, and now she's shown up to stay there for a specific reason.'

'Right. And?'

'In my mind there are two possibilities. She is also being guided by the *Huldufólk* to help you, or she knows more about the murder stuff around here than she's letting on. Or both. Maybe she'd already seen Helene's ghost before you got here? I just want to ask her the questions that you haven't.'

I'm strangely protective over Birta. The pain behind

the eyes, the way she loves to be in my company, the way I was 'chosen' by her, just like Alfvin, who warms me to the centre of my soul when he calls me 'Chosen'. I'd not thought about her knowing more than she's letting on. She hasn't given the slightest hint of it. But she has been extremely attentive to me the few times we've hung out. And she's not wanted to meet anyone else. I think about her seventies-bedecked home. She's obviously too young to have been involved in any way in the mess that went on, she'd have been a child, but maybe she's related to someone who was. Maybe she's looking for answers as much as I am.

'You know what, I'd never find her place in this fog, you're right. But if it clears, she did promise she'd come over if the porch light comes on tonight, so you can meet her then. Or I can walk you over there, hopefully. Once I can see.'

Suddenly I have that weird fluttering in my stomach again. Something is about to happen.

'Thor . . .'

'I know, I feel it. Something about being next to you heightens my instincts. It scares me as well as excites me.'

'I told you. You've got a lot of magic in you. I magnify it.'

'Check your phone, Tanz.'

I haven't even thought about my phone since we got up. It's in my hoodie pocket, a hoodie I nicked out of the cupboard. I seem to have made myself a bit too at home here. I check and there's no reception. People have been messaging constantly the past twenty-four hours and I've been ignoring them, keeping it in silent mode. Now I don't have to ignore anyone as there's now no way to reach me. 'No reception.'

'Reception went before we got up. That's not as common as you may think here. And there's this fog. It's not at all usual, not with the threatening snow. We get fog, yes, but this is "can't see thirty centimetres in front of your face" fog. It's strange.'

'Something's about to kick off, Thor. I'm glad you're here with me.'

He smiles, not looking very scared at all. Just excited.

'So am I. You're certainly not boring.'

Neil the policeman always says that. Poor Neil, what a cow I've been. He'd probably love this too. A 'proper' murder to get his teeth into.

'*Chosen.*'

I hear it, crystal clear from within the fog, only a few feet away. That unmistakable timbre. My heart leaps and Thor's expression changes to fearful wonder.

'Tanz . . . ? Did you . . . ?'

I touch his arm. 'Shhhhh . . .'

We both sit in silence and wait. Surrounded by impenetrable mist in the crisp, cold air, it becomes apparent that all birdsong has stopped, everything has stopped. Perfect, unbroken stillness. Then the voice once more.

'*Come.*'

I stand in answer and so does Thor. 'Are you hearing him in Icelandic or English, Thor?'

He whispers back. 'Icelandic. You?'

'English.'

'Fuck.'

I take Thor's hand and lead him to the rowan tree. The plate has gone. So has the pendant.

I put my fingers to my lips and we stand in reverent silence together until he speaks again. '*With thanks, Chosen and Thor. It is time. Follow.*'

My heart leaps in my chest like a startled rabbit. Thor tightens his grip.

Despite the fog, we can see a shadow ahead. Both of us. We shouldn't be able to see it but we do. It radiates light, but dark light, if that's possible. It moves away from us and a shadowy arm indicates a direction.

'*Follow.*'

Hand in hand, we do as we're told and follow the shadow into the deepest fog.

HIDDEN FOLK RAVE

Picking your way through thick fog while following a shadow is exactly as tricky as it sounds. But we move quietly and determinedly behind our guide, who seems extremely sure-footed in this landscape. For my part, walking hand in hand with Thor, I feel like I have an extra 'protection', as I seem to know when there will be a rock or a dip or a tangled root to avoid. I'm currently not as cold as I was and I do sense that we're in some kind of protective bubble. Now and then we whisper to one another just to keep a sense of normality in an extremely surreal situation.

'Tanz, this is the craziest thing that's ever happened to me and that's saying something.'

'Ditto. Plus, don't judge me, I think I'm madly in love with an elf.'

To my utter embarrassment, I hear that 'cough, cough' sound from up ahead. Alfvin's laugh. *He heard me!* Thor also laughs and says, 'Can't be any worse than being in love with Einar.'

He's not wrong. I'm glad we can joke because this really is a strange situation, and as we walk on blindly, for at least another half hour, I do wonder why Alfvin couldn't have just given us a location to find on our own. There must be a reason that he is leading us himself, under the cover of fog. (I don't believe for one bloody minute that this fog happened by coincidence.) Even as I'm thinking this, the ground beneath our feet becomes much rockier and we find ourselves negotiating an incline. Thor's hand gives my fingers an extra squeeze as we also begin to hear a rhythmic sound. It's drumming, with some kind of horn playing along. A hypnotic tune that also, as we get closer, includes voices. The chant is melodic and the voices blend to make a sound like a harmonium on the wind; far away, then suddenly close, then far again. It's a sound that hits you in the diaphragm and makes you feel everything at once.

'Thor, are they singing in Icelandic?'

'No, I don't know what language it is, but it's incredible. It sounds *old*.'

The drumming, as we get even closer to the music, mirrors the drumming I felt in the pit of my stomach when I first landed at the airport a few days ago (it feels like a month ago at the minute). Soon Alfvin's shadow stops ahead of us, before the mouth of what looks like a cave, and we also stop. There are flaming torches lit inside the cave, and dimly, far back among the rocks, we can see the shadows of *Huldufólk*, the ones that have played us up to this rocky place, and who keep playing as the mist before us dissipates enough to see, about ten feet away from the mouth of this cave or tunnel or whatever it is, a hole in the ground where rocks have been cleared and earth freshly dug. There is a flaming torch standing by the hole. About five feet away to the right is another flaming torch, harder to make out, right by another hole, I'm sure. It's pretty obvious to me what these holes will contain and suddenly I'm scared.

Alfvin steps towards the closer, larger hole, and the music comes abruptly to a halt. Then a horn sounds, once, twice. I somehow *know* it's a giant horn made of bone, and I remember hearing it before, in my dream, the dream when I first saw Alfvin. By the light of the flickering torch, in the mist which has softened ever so slightly, I can see more of his actual form. His hair is long and dark but I can detect a sheen of silver at the roots and ends. His face is long and perfectly smooth with huge eyes which still have the shimmer of starlight over them when he looks at us. His outfit resembles darkest hemp, a long jacket or shirt over loose trousers, with boots. If I stare straight at him, he half disappears, his form juddering and distorting, so I have to give him the side-eye instead. I hope he doesn't think I'm being rude. I glance at Thor, who's transfixed. Then Alfvin speaks. First, he chants in a language neither of us can discern, and at the end of each phrase, the *Huldufólk* inside the cave echo the last word in sing-song voices. It's an incredible sound. Then Alfvin turns and faces us square on. I try to see if his philtrum is indeed different to a human one, but can't entirely tell. He still looks like he's being 'masked' somehow, so we can't properly fix on him.

'*Chosen. You come to free innocents who were left here. Helene has begged to be seen. And at last, after many years, you saw. Now she can be reunited with her son. Her family will have answers. And a lost soul, wandering, ever wandering, can make her way home.'*

His eyes then fix on Thor.

'Thor. Friend of Chosen. You will keep Huldufólk *land safe. No trespassers here. We will dig holes closer to your home tonight, put earth from here in them. Match the bones. But before, Chosen must do her magic at the burial ground.'*

Thor nods. I'm a bit confused but I think I follow. It has to be here that I 'clear' Helene and Paul. This is where they were dumped. It's sad that they were buried so close together and yet she couldn't 'find' him. Probably because she was still earth-bound by trauma, and he, as a small innocent child, was not.

I pat Thor's arm, to let him know to stay put, then step forward, ready to look into the first hole. My bottom lip begins to wobble as I get within a few feet of Alfvin. Just knowing he exists moves me beyond all comprehension, and his presence brings out so much yearning and love in me. As I carefully approach, stopping a couple of feet away from him, he touches his large graceful hand to his breastbone, and I see the amethyst on the black cord hanging from his neck. I nod into his starlit eyes and he reaches forward and, to my absolute shock, 'boops' my nose. It makes me laugh, and I 'feel' his smile in response. After a few moments he gives a slight bow and I watch as he retreats to the mouth of the cave and sits on a rock. The shadow figures inside keep far back but are all looking my way, I can tell by the sets of silvered eyes glinting in the firelight. I step towards the hole, and see white bones sticking out. This is Helene, I know it is. I walk to the other hole, and see the smaller, heartbreaking bones of a child. Guided by my gut instinct and that deep buried voice that speaks at the most crucial of times, I squat and pick up Paul's tiny skull. I then walk back to where Helene lies and very delicately place it next to her skull, which has been carefully cleared of soil and debris by these extraordinary beings.

Then I stand, put my hands together as in prayer, and close my eyes.

'Helene and Paul, beautiful souls, you have been hidden from the world and from each other for so long. Now you are reunited and your story will be told. I'm so sorry that a horrible man who was meant to protect you ended your lives violently instead. I know a good man called Ernest who will tell your family and the rest of the world everything about what happened. You are not forgotten and never will be. Please be at peace.'

When I open my eyes Helene is standing, semi solid, at the other side of the hole, looking down.

'Is that me?'

'It is. I'm so sorry. And that little skull, that's Paul's.'

Tears are rolling down her face. 'Jack won't let me see him.'

'Jack is not with you, Helene. That's your fear, that's why you suddenly hear him roaring at you sometimes. I heard it too when we were talking and you disappeared. That was the last sound you heard from him as he fired the gun. But I promise, he's not with you or around you. He died in another country. And you don't have to think of him, or protect him any more. You didn't even let me see his face. That's because you were still terrified of what he could do to you. Well, no more. Look over there, Helene.'

As I'm talking, I notice a flicker of blue light to her left. It grows until it's the outline of a door. Before I even see it, I know what will happen next. A little boy's head peeks around the door frame, the biggest smile on his face. Helene's cry when she sees him is almost anguished.

'Paul?'

He steps back and holds out his arms. Without even looking at me she runs to him, and stoops to scoop him up. I hear the delighted laugh of a child and just like that, the blue light disappears and they're gone. I've seen this before: the earth-bound often disappear in the blink of an eye when they see 'the light'. I turn to the mouth of the cave and nod to Alfvin, who slowly stands and bows, then chants something in that beautiful, incomprehensible language. Then the 'folk' in the cave echo him and begin to play their music again, the drumming louder than ever. Just then I notice a shadowy figure emerging from the cave and walking towards Thor. This one feels more feminine. She puts her hand on his face and he gazes at her in wonder. Alfvin grabs a flaming torch and walks back towards me.

'Home.'

The figure by Thor bows lightly then walks back to the cave. I take his hand.

'I think it's time to leave now, Thor.'

He gazes at me, tears running down his face, then

breaks into a grin. 'I met her again. And now I'm fucking destroyed.'

'Come on, you big soft shite.'

I'm not going to let on to him, but I'm exhausted. I don't usually do ghost-busts on my own anyway, but this was something else. And with an audience like that as well. Magic beings watching me do my 'magic'. Like anyone needs that kind of pressure. The music dies down to a hum now, like a sweet goodbye lullaby. I wish I could sit among these ancients and learn even something of the knowledge that they hold, but if they wanted to share that, they would, I'm sure. Up ahead, the mist is thick as all hell again and all I can see is a shadow and a flaming torch, waiting for us to move. Just as I'm about to walk towards Alfvin I feel a light touch on my back and turn. From the mist two extremely delicate hands emerge holding small shot glasses, just like Thor proffered last night before I talked with Helene. The 'being' holding out the drinks is as light as gossamer, almost transparent, in this once again thick-as-all-hell fog. I wonder if it's an elder or a child? I pass a glass to Thor.

'*Drink,*' is all I hear, from a voice like a woodwind instrument. We do as we're told, and both down these small tots of earthy, dark liquid. To my surprise, it's like a pleasant shot of burned black toffee and as soon as it hits my stomach I'm not tired any more. Not seeing anyone around us to hand them back to, we place the empty glasses on the ground and Thor smacks his lips.

'I don't know what that was but I liked it!'

He sounds as energized as I suddenly am. We grab each other and turn towards the flaming torch that is now moving purposely back the way we came. Or I hope it's back the way we came. How would I bloody know when I can't see more than three feet ahead through the fog? But as we pick our way downhill and back over the moss, I feel as safe as I could in the circumstances. And like my life just altered for ever.

BACK TO THE REAL WORLD

Back at the cabin I can hear my mobile phone ringing before I'm properly through the door. I left it on the table, which just shows how distracted I've been, seeing as that thing is glued to me when I'm in London.

Thor and I are buzzing right now. How is anyone meant to process what just happened? Plus, whatever was in that shot of elf juice has completely woken us up. When we got within a short walk of this place, Alfvin stopped dead and we heard his voice loud and clear:

'*Tomorrow at noon you will feel the calling. Bones will be revealed in their new burial place, not far from here. When asked, that is where they were found. The* Huldufólk *thank you, Chosen and Thor.*'

Before either of us could say a damn thing, his flaming torch snuffed out. Simply disappeared, as did his energy. Just gone. And within two minutes, in front of our incredulous eyes, the fog retreated back to the hills, revealing the cabin in the distance, all lights ablaze in the fading light. Obviously we hadn't left the lights on today when we left, but we also didn't question it. We were way past anything surprising us by that point.

And now I look at that little screen and don't recognize the number. I nearly don't answer, then a nagging feeling tells me I should.

'Tanz, hello, it's Ernest. I've found out some very interesting new facts about the case. How are things your end?'

'Well, Ernest, I think I may just have something to show you at noon tomorrow.'

'Any chance of us meeting up? I think you might like these missing pieces of the jigsaw. They rather back up what you told me this morning.'

I look at Thor, who's put the coffee on but is watching me on the phone, hands fidgeting, obviously not knowing what to do with himself.

'Thor, should we drive back to town and meet with Ernest? We can have a drink and he can tell us his new discoveries. It might be good to let off some steam.'

'Fuck, yes. Give me the phone, I'll tell him where Ölstafa is. We can meet there in two hours.'

The lad looks very relieved and, truthfully, so am I. I'm bursting with what just happened. Obviously the *Huldufólk* stuff is not for Ernest's ears, but at least we can give him some info for Helene's niece. Not the nicest news for her, but she'll get closure and the satisfaction of Helene and Paul not just being forgotten people.

Within a short time he's off the phone again and handing it to me.

'I'm going to call Gunnar and give him my shifts tomorrow. Then let's get on the road. We need a night in a bar.'

A WITCH, A WIZARD, A P.I. AND A C*NT

Thor very kindly brought me to the little place he found for me to stay, and let me grab a quick shower and a change of clothes. I was kneeling by a grave earlier so it's only right I put on something with clean knees. He grabbed a shower after me and I used the time to put on some make-up. The northern working-class girl in me was not going to the pub without putting my face on and dousing myself in good perfume. I also watered his friend's plants, which was only fair. I may not have stayed there yet but they still needed it.

Now we're sitting at a wooden table in Ölstafa with a pink tea-light glowing on it and this first G&T is going down a treat. It's not rammed here but pleasantly full and by the sounds of it, a bunch of the customers are American tourists, but there are seemingly a lot of locals too, which is always a good sign. There's a smoking bit to this pub that's like a large greenhouse at the side and there are lots of people in there, chatting animatedly. They certainly like their cigarettes over here. Thor talked a lot on the drive back about how meeting me has made his 'dream come true' that he'd one day meet the lady who saved him. Before Ernest gets here, I decide to expand on what I think has happened since he met me. I keep my voice down as it's really not for everyone's ears.

'Thor, I think you need to realize something. No matter how much I can spread and share my energy, another person can't "see" extra stuff without having the talent lying in them already. You saw Helene standing by the hole today, right?'

'I saw a transparent woman, yes. Like a hologram. It was very strange. Then she disappeared.'

'Yes, and you saw the Hidden Folk in the cave, you saw your special saviour lady and you could see Alfvin. All shadowy but definitely there.'

'Yes.' The look of joy as he says it is a sight to behold.

'You're a wizard. As much as I'm a witch, you're a wizard, whatever those terms actually mean in the modern world, and you were ready to be "activated" when you met me. You were ready but didn't know how to go about it. Just like you were sent to me to facilitate me in finding and helping Helene, I was sent to you, so you could go to the next level. You're not scared of it now. You've experienced how normal it can feel to experience the extraordinary. It takes a bit of getting used to, but once you're open like this, anything can happen. You are a magic one, you just needed to stand next to someone else with the same energy to actually move into that space. I'm so happy for you . . .'

He virtually glows when I say this. Before I can say anything else, Ernest appears at the table, in a salmon shirt and the same stained tie. He's wearing a gigantic Icelandic cardigan too, which almost makes me laugh. He's looking mighty pleased with himself, it has to be said. Thor jumps up.

'Sit down, Ernest, and let me get you a drink.'

'Very kind of you. I'll have a pale ale, please.'

'Coming up.'

Thor goes to the bar, which is round and in the middle of the room, and where he seems to know every single member of staff. He turns and points at my drink. It's half gone so I nod, seeing as he's at the bar anyway.

'So, Ernest, you've been a busy boy today?'

'I have indeed. A lot of phone calls, a bit of digging, a lucky break while chatting in a coffee shop down the road. Also, a near heart attack when I saw how much it cost for a sandwich and a packet of crisps.'

'Oh, yeah, nothing's cheap around here. I found that out when I got drinks at Lebowski Bar. I'd probably have to get a bank loan to go out on a pub crawl here.'

He laughs, then looks down at a little notepad he's brought with him. Thor returns, having been served before everyone else, a perk of knowing absolutely every resident in Reykjavík.

'So, are you two ready for the missing bits of the puzzle? You both seem to be rather perky tonight.'

I laugh at this. 'We are indeed. We had an interesting day too. We'll tell you afterwards, but first you. Come on. Spill.'

Thor is sitting next to me, and puts his knee against my leg as Ernest, sitting opposite, begins to speak. I understand this compulsion completely. It makes it very hard not to want to be close to someone when you've shared the experience we did today. I don't budge, but let my leg relax against his.

'So first things first. I wanted to know when "Jack" left Iceland, working on your theory that when he left here, his wife and child weren't with him. Estate agents now weren't going to be able to help with rentals that went on in 1976 so I couldn't ask when the property was vacated. That property isn't even standing any more – Thor's house is built on top of it, basically – but I called a contact of mine who managed to locate the last effects of Jack Thomas, by then known as Lewis Stevens. Where he lived when he died was pretty isolated, a small farmhouse in a village in Ireland with one shop and one pub. He got in a fight in that pub with a younger lad and came off worse when he took a punch and smacked his head against a table. Never recovered. Anyway, the place he lived was a rental, and it sounds like it was in a pretty similar state to the place he rented here. Stone walls, damp, run-down. The landlord was elderly and didn't touch it. When my contact found it, he was directed into the attic, which still held rubbish from thirty years of tenants. There was plenty of mildew, but two old suitcases that were still there held everything Lewis Stevens owned when he died. My contact has those effects now, after slipping the owner a few quid, and one of the things he found was a boat ticket from 1976. From Iceland to Denmark in the name of Jack Thomas. It was dated six months after he arrived in Iceland with his family; that's documented from Carol's end. They left in March. It looks like he made his way back to Blighty incrementally, via Denmark. The letter he sent to Helene's family from Ireland came two months after that. It stands to reason that if he was avoiding the law in England, he would take a back-door route coming back. And it doesn't look like he ever actually got any closer than Ireland. And it also doesn't look like his wife and son left here with him.'

All of this makes me so sad. Such a bloody waste. I shake my head and sip more gin. 'What a dark, horrible life he lived.'

'Indeed. My contact also had a conversation with an old boy in a pub, while he was there. He bought him a bunch of drinks and told him Jack was his long-lost uncle, that he'd come to see the place he'd lived and died. My contact mentioned the following conversation at the time but it could have been about any of the women Jack had been with. He liked to spread his seed and then run away, it seems, so I didn't take as much notice as I maybe should have. I wrote it all down, though, and it would certainly make sense now, if you really do have an insight that the rest of us don't.'

He doesn't say this unkindly. He looks at me appraisingly over his pale ale and I think he believes in me more than he lets on.

'He said Jack was drunk one night and started to cry and said, "I met my true love over the sea. The most passionate woman you'd ever encounter. And then that whore discovered us; screamed at me, said she'd tell all and ruin my chance at love. I had to shut her up. How dare she try to destroy my one chance? But the boy ran in straight after the gun went off, caught me off guard. It was an accident.

My love would have loved him too, I'm sure of it. But that whore ruined everything. I hope she rots in a different hell to me, because that's surely where I'm going." The old boy said he didn't know what he was talking about, and didn't want to know either, but it was the only time he saw "Lewis" show any emotion apart from anger. Lewis was an angry man, he said, always ready to take offence. But he'd cried about this mystery woman and the boy he'd hurt by accident.'

The emotion of this news makes me feel sick. I stare down at the table as one tear, then another runs down my face. Thor strokes the back of my neck and Ernest stares into his drink until I gather myself and smile up at him.

'This is all incredible, Ernest, your contact is amazing. And now I need to say something out loud which includes some of my spooky stuff, if that's okay?'

Thor smiles encouragingly. He's all for the spooky stuff. Ernest nods. 'In for a penny . . .'

'Well, I know it's assuming a lot, but everything else that's happened to me since I got here has tied in, and in a dream I had – well, more of a vision really – I saw two lovers entwined extremely passionately, and felt the anguish of another woman, who was watching them. I can only assume this was Helene, witnessing her husband's infidelity. Even in the dream I could see how into each other those two lovers were, sexually at least. If he felt he'd met his "true love" and the wife had got in the way, that would explain what he did, in a twisted way. But it leaves the conundrum of why he left soon after, alone. Surely if he went to the trouble of killing his wife and accidentally killing his son, then hiding the bodies, he would have then at least attempted to be with the lover he was so besotted with?'

Ernest nods, and turns to another page in his notebook, a small smile playing around the edges of his mouth.

'Well, this could explain it. As I said, a lucky break in a coffee shop down the road. I got talking to this older man who was on his own at the next table. I introduced myself and said I'd been looking for a "Jack" who came here for a bit in 1976, that it was for inheritance purposes as he was next in line for a bob or two. The man said that he didn't know him but that there had been farm buildings dotted about in the seventies in the area I was talking about and that his brother had been a builder, contracted by this guy, Gisli, who owned a few, to level the worst one and renovate others that could at least partly be salvaged. They weren't all falling down but a bunch of them were in a state of disrepair. He'd had a shock, this Gisli, when a lady tenant in one of his buildings had killed herself. Made her way to the cliffs and jumped off. It was low tide and someone found her before she was washed away. Suicide rates in those days weren't exactly low apparently, but still, this Gisli saw it as some kind of dark omen because she wasn't that old and was a nice person, so he wanted to fix up and sell up. And that's what he did. When pressed, the man in the coffee shop reckoned it was probably 1976 because he remembered hearing about it when his youngest son had just been born. His son was born at the end of August 1976. He couldn't remember the woman's full name but he thought her first name was Kristin.'

This makes me feel a little dizzy. This could be why

I saw the man with 'secrets' staring over the cliff in my dream. I had huge feelings about someone jumping. Could it be he was contemplating where his lover had died, rather than thinking of jumping himself? If so, it would tie up most of the loose ends of this awful, pointless murder that happened. But then why does it feel so unfinished? I don't have that sense of completion that I've had before when I 'solved' things. It's Thor the newly hatched wizard who pipes up here.

'Tanz. Tell him about Birta.'

'Why?'

I see Ernest's ears prick up. 'Who's that?'

I roll my eyes. 'There's a lady who lives about half a mile from Thor's place. In a farm building that's still standing. Leaky but still solid, and it's done out like a museum to the seventies. She's an artist so it's no big surprise, and there are plenty of her paintings and pottery there too. Plus, she's had a lot of shit from men so she keeps herself to herself. She showed up and saved me during the power cut, and helped give me energy and back-up so I could talk to Helene. She's as much of a spooky woman as I am and Thor doesn't believe she's just a random person living under the radar.'

Ernest nods. 'How old is she?'

'Not much older than me. She'd have been too young to have been involved in anything in 1976, just a child.'

Thor pipes up. 'She showed up just when the ghostly activity really kicked off around my house. She also came back to help Tanz when I was there. I saw her in the dark with her lantern, but she refused to come in and meet me. I just think it's a bit off. I think she's also looking for something, and has a link to all of this.'

Ernest takes a slug of his almost-finished beer and regards me through slightly steamed-up lenses.

'Tanz, I'm going to use the language you just used. You said that everything that's happened to you since you got here has all "tied in". I'm not going to categorically state that I believe in all of your spooky stuff, but on a factual basis you've not got it wrong as far as I can see, about anything you told me. Including names and dates. So going on *your* logic, this lady who has come to your aid, been there at the right time, right place, and lives in a building that tallies with the timeline of this saga, is almost definitely going to be "tied in" with the story. I'm going to come right out and ask it. Is it possible, by some quirk of parallel universes, that she is Kristin's niece who is trying to find out the truth of her aunt's death, just like my client? Or even her daughter, maybe Kristin had a child? Do you think she knows something extra about this suicide that could shed more light? It would certainly make my client very happy to have as much information as possible.'

Thor nods. 'That's what I was thinking. I don't like to say I "feel" it, because that's Tanz's realm, but I sense there's an extra element here that will come from Birta. Ernest, you have to come to the summer house tomorrow. Before noon. It's very important. And after that, we should go and visit Birta. I know you care for her, Tanz, we'll hang back in the car once we find her. But she knows something, I'm sure of it!'

He's making sense. There's no point denying it. He

motions to a lad at the bar, who winks and starts pouring another round of drinks for us. I sigh and admit defeat.

'Okay, we'll go and find her tomorrow. She was going to maybe pop over tonight, she said, but what with all the excitement we had today I forgot. Just let me go ahead and do the talking, please, when we get to her place. She doesn't deserve to lose her privacy just because of me.'

Ernest looks at me when I say this, probably about to ask what 'excitement' we had today, but just then I hear a familiar voice. Loud, enthusiastic and drunk. I look up and there he stands, a straggle-haired giant in his vampire clothes, laughing animatedly with a man and two women who were already sitting at the bar. Thor clocks him at the same second.

'Uh-oh. Tanz, let me . . .'

I'm out of my seat before he can finish. I stand next to the drunken liar, and give a little tug on his shirt. He looks down at me from his great height and blinks twice.

'Hello, Einar.'

Einar hardly misses a beat as I stare up at him defiantly. 'Hello, beautiful woman.' He turns to the people he's talking to, and grins expansively. 'This is Tanz. She's a gorgeous Geordie from the north of England. And I think she wants to punch me.'

I cannot fucking believe the gall of this man. Thor is by my side now, and taps his card on the machine to pay for our drinks.

'Einar, don't be a dick.'

Einar looks at him, abashed, then at me. 'Tanz, may I speak with you, please? I owe you an explanation.'

'I already know everything I need to know, Einar. What a fucking horrible way to treat another human being.'

He takes a shot of whisky that's waiting in front of him and downs it fast.

'Tanz, I am a cunt. This is well known. Allow me five minutes of your time in the smoking room. Thor, you can see us from there. Please. Just five minutes.'

Thor looks like he's going to tell him to fuck off, but I take his arm at the elbow and look into his eyes. 'It's okay, I'll be back in a minute. You keep Ernest company and I'll buy us the next round. You've spent enough already.'

Thor nods and hands me my drink.

'You know what you're doing, my witchy friend.'

I wink at him and follow Einar out to a tiny two-seater table that's squashed into a corner. Everything else is taken. We sit and Einar bends forward, beer in hand, intent on no one else hearing what he has to say, obviously.

'I wasn't totally honest with you.'

'You weren't honest with me at all.'

He looks into my eyes, pouring every ounce of warm charm and sorrow into his stare.

'I'm a naughty boy, Tanz, but not in the way you think. I did not lie. I did fancy you on sight in Hampstead. I also took you to dinner because you were so gorgeous and interesting. I did think you were the sexiest woman in the world while we danced naked. I love how you kiss and how you think about the world and how alive you are.'

'And you also have a long-term girlfriend.'

'I do and she's a pain in the fucking ass.'

'A pain for finding you out or a pain for making you accountable? Where is she now? What are you doing here?'

'She ran away from work to come and chew my ear off. She's had to fly back now, to make up for lost hours. It's ridiculous.'

'She obviously loves you, Einar. What's ridiculous about that?'

'I'm a libertine, Tanz. I don't want to cut off new stories as they appear, simply to keep the old story happy. I need to be free!'

'So why be in a relationship with her then? Finish it.'

'Life's not that simple. Why can't she just be happy for me?'

'*Happy for you*? Happy that you meet other people and pretend to be single? What about me, Einar? Why the hell did you invite me here?'

'I told you. I did tell you, the other night, that I only do wonderful affairs. I *told* you not to get attached.'

'That's not *quite* what you told me. You also told me that London was an easy commute and that you were hoping to do more of it since you met me. You may have said you only do affairs but then you *implied* that you wanted more.'

'I didn't mean to imply that. I just wanted you to know that I found you very attractive and I admired your bravery for flying out here.'

'Yes, I think maybe that caught you off guard a bit.'

Einar's eyes are glazing over. Who knows how much he's had to drink already but whisky followed by a beer has fully taken him to squiffy-town, which in a way is good as I get the truth. He slams his now empty bottle down on the table and nods emphatically while waving one finger in the air.

'YES! I was surprised. It was courageous, it was what a free and unafraid woman would do. But WHY are you so mad now, that I'm not a man to be pinned down? You got your place to stay and write, you are having an adventure, ARE YOU NOT?!'

I should hate him but I almost want to laugh. I've been saved a terrible heartache. This man, with his ducking and diving and completely self-centred way of looking at things, could have smashed my heart into twelve million pieces if I'd not had my eyes opened so rudely, and so quickly. I look through the window to where Ernest and Thor are drinking and they're watching me back. Thor has a darkness in his eyes I've not seen before. It takes me a second to register what it is. He's angry, and if I'm not mistaken, he's jealous. Oh my goodness. My newly hatched wizard has a touch of the green-eyed monster.

'Einar, yes, I have those things. And all of them, everything special I've experienced and enjoyed in the past few days, has been directly because of Thor. His vehicle, his house, his kindness, his time, his brilliance.'

'Thor is my friend!' He sounds a little petulant now. Like he's gutted that he upset Thor, not me. It hits me then, Thor is his true love, that's what this is about. Einar needs women like he needs shiny baubles. He needs to be affirmed, adored and sexually desired, for his ego and his insecurities. But Thor, Thor is the true rock in his life. Now

I get it. Einar needs family, that's what he values. Women are just his pretty walking sticks to lean on. I stand up.

'I'm off to get drunk with your friend, Einar. Have a good night.'

I don't even wait for a reply, I just go back to Thor and Ernest.

'Drink up, boys. Let's go somewhere else away from here.'

Ernest shakes his head, stands and puts on a padded jacket over the big cardigan that I suspect he just bought. Heaven knows how expensive it was.

'I have another report to write up. But you two go ahead and have a good night. I'll drive to the summer house by half past eleven tomorrow morning, if that suits?'

Thor nods. 'Perfect. We'll see you there.'

Ernest exits and I'm left with Thor, and a wounded-looking Einar who is standing at the bar, getting more whisky no doubt.

'Thor, go and speak to him, he's getting absolutely wrecked. You're his best friend and I think he really is sorry that he upset you.'

'Of course he is. I've put up with his shit for years and even he knows this is worse behaviour than usual. Don't worry about him being drunk by the way, this is his natural state. He'll take something to balance it soon, then go to the casino. This is the night just starting for him.'

I look up at Einar, stooped over his drink, eyes red, skin slightly livid from lack of sleep and booze, and now I just see a lucky escape. Then I look at Thor and see the type of person I should always wait for. One who is kind to me without being asked, a gentleman, someone with his own life, his own passions and, best of all, an empath. I'd want the single version, though. No more men who already have someone.

MUSIC STARS AND WIZARDS

Thor puts his arm around me and leads me down to a street by the harbour. I'm feeling slightly tipsy, but more than that, I'm just overwhelmed by everything that's happened today. He knocks on a door and suddenly we're in someone's living room but it's not, it's a bar, with twinkly lights, little double sofas and tiny tables. The guy who lets us in is tall and black with a large oiled afro and a gorgeous smile. He hugs Thor and shakes my hand. Thor introduces him as Emil. We sit by the window on two comfy chairs, with a tiny table between us and a view of the sea.

'Holy fuck, Thor, this is amazing.'

He winks at me as we hear two cocktails being prepared by a girl behind the bar. Soon the drinks are placed in front of us by Emil, with a bowl of olives. 'Hey, you've bought enough drinks. This was supposed to be my round.'

He puts his finger to his lips. 'This is my friend's place, only open to people he knows. My treat as a thank you for changing my life around. This drink is one of their specialities. Tell me what you think.'

'Oh my God, it's tasty! What is it?'

'Rhubarb mojito. It has a secret ingredient he won't tell anyone. Delicious, yes?'

'It really is lovely. Thank you, Thor. You're a whole box of fantastic surprises.'

All at once I feel shy. He looks at his drink, and keeps looking at it while he talks.

'I hated you talking to Einar tonight.'

'I could tell.'

'I'm not the jealous type and I have a girlfriend. Or kind of a girlfriend. But I just . . . He did nothing to earn you. Nothing to earn the huge, amazing energy that you have. The magic. The love. I try not to judge him, I know how damaged he is. But he walks away from women, and you are not someone to be walked away from. I wanted to hit him in his alcoholic's nose.'

I break out into laughter here and he joins in. Emil comes over.

'What am I missing?' His accent is beautiful, his voice like silk.

'She met Einar. He charmed her but I think it's worn off now.'

'Oh no, don't be charmed by Einar. Like dancing with a snake. He'll turn around and bite you, then slither away to the next one. You're far too good for Einar.'

I don't understand why everyone is being so nice to me. I stare at Emil. His perfect dark skin. His stunning eyes.

'Excuse me, Emil, I'm a tad tipsy, but you look like a

rock star. And your voice sounds so smooth. You must be a singer.'

He smiles and bends to whisper in my ear. 'You might be right, but don't tell anybody.' Then he moves off, laughing to himself.

'Okay, Thor, what am I missing here?'

'In this country Emil is well known as a singer. This is his sideline. He likes people, and everyone needs extra money. But only friends are welcome.'

'This place is crazy. Music stars running bars from their living rooms, wizards driving tour buses . . .'

'I have to tell you, you've confused me, Tanz.'

'How?'

'I'm careful these days. Watchful of people, especially women. But you've bypassed all of that. You say what you mean, you don't seem to lie, you don't play games, and insane, cool shit happens around you. Now I don't want to be around anyone else, and you're flying back to England soon. What will I do then?'

'You'll get on with your life, see your girlfriend, do your job, and know that something amazing, or spooky, or crazy could happen at any time. And you'll be open to it.'

'But it won't be as much fun without you. Nothing will be as much fun without you.'

'You'd change your mind if you spent more time around me.'

He shakes his head, runs his hand through his tawny red beard.

'I wouldn't. I know I wouldn't. We could learn so much together. Today, while you stood there and told a trapped spirit she could go with her son, the light changed. I promise you, it got lighter as you finished and they left. Then my rescuer, my Hidden One, came to me, and she touched my face, and suddenly I knew that even less mattered in this life than I thought, and everything that's happened to me was just to make me stronger. Then I looked at you, and I saw your pain. It was like a purple light, strength and love, with pain. And I wanted to make you better. But I don't know how, and how can I learn if you don't even live here?'

'I . . . wow . . .'

'What we did today. What happened, and what they told us. All of it, it was so much more special than just hanging out with someone and being attracted to them. It meant something, it changed things, it redressed a balance that others don't even know about. I want to be of help like that for ever. I want to be of service. But I wish I could do it with you there.'

God, he's being so lovely. And for once in my life it feels equal. We've not touched each other sexually, we've been respectful and chatty and we've done spooky stuff in tandem and held each other close when necessary. I think this is how you're supposed to get to know people before you get intimate. Find out if you work as friends. Of course I've only been here a few days, so it's still far too early to tell if we could actually gel as partners, but it has made me think about how I choose people. Usually, I talk with someone, I get a sexual spark and pretty much instantaneously after that it's take-your-clothes-off time.

'Thor, you have a partner, and I have fancied a drunken, gambling loon, then my female artist friend—'

'What? You fancy Birta?'

'I don't know if it's fancy actually. I've been thinking about it and its weird. It's like I've known her for hundreds of years and the familiarity makes me feel things that I normally wouldn't. I'm very aware of her voice, her scent and how it is when I hug her. I'm also very protective of her. What the hell is that?'

'I remember my dad talking about this. He used to study all kinds of strange things. Do you know that when members of families are separated at a young age, or for a huge amount of time, like brothers and sisters, fathers and daughters, mothers and sons et cetera, when they meet again for the first time, the pull can be so strong they end up being sexual together? Maybe you really do know her from a past life, so you have this irresistible pull when you see her.'

'What a thought. It would actually explain a few things. But it's also crazy, even by my standards, and I salute you for suggesting it!'

I think the special shot from the *Huldufólk* is wearing off now as I'm exhausted. The same lethargy seems to have just hit Thor, as all at once he slumps in his chair.

'Tanz, I'm suddenly very, very tired.'

'Well, we need to be back at the summer house by eleven thirty tomorrow so maybe it's time to sleep off today's adventures.'

He nods and we slowly stumble our way back to my little studio. When we reach the door and I fumble the key out of my bag, I turn to Thor and put my hand on his face, like the Hidden One did earlier tonight.

'Shouldn't you go and stay with your lady now?'

'Absolutely not. She had a date with another woman tonight. And I just want to sleep next to my Geordie goddess. I promise I'll behave.'

He's much more of a gentleman than I am. Luckily we're so bone-weary when we climb into the cute double bed in the cosy little bedroom that within a minute of him snuggling up close we're both fast asleep without a dream between us.

MISS BOSSY PANTS

We've both been a little preoccupied during the drive back to the cabin. Not the usual jokey chatter for us. We don't know where the Hidden Folk are going to put the bones and how they'll tell us. That's nerve-racking in itself. Plus, there's suddenly a wall up between us. We've spent days happily in each other's pockets, but now we can't 'be' with each other. I'm off home soon and won't be able to just hang out with him, and he has a girlfriend anyway. Usually I'm so impetuous with men but not this time; I have to be a grown-up and it sucks. We woke up together this morning, cuddled up yet again, and it was so hard not to melt into him. I didn't do it, though, because I can't be bloody trusted with my choices, I've not properly finished with Neil yet, and just once I have to do the right thing.

Thor prepares us coffee as I pace the living room of the summer house. It's 11.10 a.m. and Alfvin said they'd send a sign at noon. Obviously elf time's weird, or they have different clocks because Thor nearly drops the coffee pot when suddenly there's the sound of a giant bone horn blowing from outside. It's so loud it doesn't feel like the windows are closed.

'What the hell, Thor?'

His face crinkles at me. 'I love the drama. It's like a Viking movie.'

We open the door to the stoop and the horn sounds again. It's loud but the direction it's coming from is easily discernible. It's a little beyond the patch of bushes where I spoke to Helene's crying ghost. We walk towards it together and just behind the bushes is a cleared patch of ground with a fresh hole dug, earth left around the sides. From what I can see, the bones have been mixed with soil and are in two piles in the hole, roughly in the shape they would have been buried. No sign of Alfvin, which is disappointing, but I couldn't imagine him showing up in plain sight with the sky bright like this anyway.

We both stand by the edge of this new grave, and even though the bones have been moved from somewhere else, it's hard not to choke up. Two people who didn't need to die, left in the cold ground for all that time, being guarded by a race of beings I would never have dared believe in.

'Thor. Why now?'

He takes my hand and there's a jolt of energy. He truly has been 'activated'. He's every bit as sensitive as I am, I'm sure of it.

'Ernest. He was looking. The niece wanted answers, and "they" needed someone to sort everything out, reunite Helene's restless spirit with Paul and release her trapped soul. Then they could move the bones from *Huldufólk* land

and stop the police from trampling where they live. They're very protective of their space.'

'Yes, I remember Alfvin telling me that. So we had to get there before anyone bumbled into the truth, you think?'

'You had to, not "we". I've just been a lucky passenger. They couldn't move the bones until you'd made things right. But it was also just the right time for some reason, and who better to sort things than a fantastic witch like you? In the magical realm you must have a beacon flashing over your head, attracting all kinds of attention.'

'First of all, you haven't been a passenger, you've facilitated every step of this journey. And the Hidden Ones showed themselves to you too, so you're no assistant, you're my equal. Second, you're also going to find a lot of spooky attention coming your way from now on, make no mistake.'

'I'm not sure that's true, Tanz, it's you who lights me up. Without you next to me, I doubt I'll be as open to all of this.'

'We'll see.'

Just then there's the sound of a car pulling up the driveway and we walk round the side to meet Ernest, in a mint-green shirt, the usual stained tie and padded jacket, and a newly acquired hat with flaps over the ears, which, like the cardigan, almost makes me laugh out loud. Instead of laughing, I smile and I give him a hug, which he doesn't know how to handle at all. It's like hugging a post box.

'Ernest. Thor and I have something to show you. It's just round the back.'

We walk him to the hole and he stares down at the

half-exposed bones, face serious, then turns to me and Thor and clears his throat.

'Well, well, well. What a convenient burial place.'

Thor nods. 'Who'd have thought it would be so close by?'

Ernest fixes his pale eyes on mine. 'So, Tanz, how did we come to find these bones?'

'Well, Ernest, you came to ask us some questions, then you and Thor went for a little hunt around outside. You were acting on a tip-off from an old builder maybe? I'm sure you can come up with something.'

'How about you? What was your involvement?'

'No involvement from me, Ernest. I was just visiting the summer house trying to write something. A casual friend of Thor's is all.'

Thor looks at me and I see such a flash of emotion in those eyes, like the shadow of storm clouds chasing each other across a wilderness, that I suddenly feel like I have to protect him with all my might. I know I'm a natural helper and I always want to save everybody, but he's shown himself to be utterly capable, a person who doesn't need saving, and yet here I am, resisting the urge to take him in my arms and make him feel better. God, I'm a sap. Iceland has turned my bloody head, I swear.

Ernest nods. 'Are Helene and Paul both in that hole?'

It sounds horrible when he puts it like that.

'They are indeed.'

He nods again. 'I would have loved to have seen where they were actually buried, you secretive pair of so-and-sos.'

I keep my face deadpan. 'I have no idea what you mean.

But speaking hypothetically, if those bones did happen to have come from somewhere else, I can guarantee you Thor and I wouldn't know how to find it.'

'Roger that.'

A shot of energy hits my belly just then and I look to Thor to see if he feels it. He looks back at me quizzically, obviously not getting this one.

'I'll tell you what, much as I hate disturbing her, I'm now getting a very strong feeling that we need to call on Birta. She's the key to the final bit of the puzzle. The lover who committed suicide. I know it doesn't matter either way in the grand scheme of things but I'd like to know why it happened and I think she'll be able to tell us. Also, I'd like to tell her that the bones have been found and Helene is at peace. Birta helped me with that, the night Helene's ghost showed me what she'd been through. On a side note, I'd also like to force her into getting a phone, Thor, because I'm going to bloody miss her. If I sent one over from London, just a brick, could you take it to her?'

'Well, we've got to see if she hates me first. You said she's sick of men, she mightn't want me calling round. Plus, we have to check if you and your ridiculous sense of direction can actually find where she lives.'

'Shut up, you, I'll use my witchy sonar! You coming, Ernest? We can drive most of the way, then we can cut through the little wood. Shouldn't take too long?'

'Well, I would, but if she's shy, maybe I should stay here and guard the graves until you're back. You can tell me what she said, then we have to think about informing the police. We can't leave the remains uncovered for too long, it'll look suspicious that we didn't call it in.'

Thor points through to the kitchen. 'All good points. There's plenty of tea through there, Ernest. And lots of things in the fridge if you fancy a snack?'

'Excellent. Well, I'll write a little report and come up with an excuse for finding the bones, shall I?'

This all sounds great to me and I give him another quick hug. 'Thank you for being okay about all of this, Ernest. I know you don't like loose threads and holes in stories, but there are aspects so crazy about all of this, I truly can't say them out loud. The main thing is that your client will find out the truth about her family members, and two innocent people who were murdered and hidden away are now found, and their stories can be told. I hope you get a bonus for being so diligent.'

'I don't want a bonus for things I didn't do. That's not how I work. You and Thor deserve most of the credit for this, I just did some background work. I'm what I think is referred to as "old school". I like credit to be given where credit's due.'

'That's because you're a good person. Now come on, Thor, let's see what Birta has to say. I really feel strongly that she wants to talk to me. And don't be pissed off if I make you sit in the Jeep for a bit at first, she needs warning that there's an extra visitor.'

'Okay, Miss Bossy Pants. Let's go.'

SISTER WITCH

It's such a beautiful day. There may only be a few hours of light here at the moment but today the sky is clear, the air is bracing and the sun is smiling down. Thor is quiet as we drive the half mile down the road to where Birta and I veered off that first morning, over mossy ground and then through a copse of bushy trees. I can actually see some kind of roof showing beyond them, only just. I point it out and we drive up a straggly path, which has been made by the wheels of other vehicles. I hadn't noticed this driveable pathway before, skirting round the trees. Thor stops the Jeep.

'Do you want me to drive to her door and risk annoying her?'

'I think we can take a gamble on it being fine. You're a fellow magic person.' But as he pulls off again and we slowly advance past the wood, I spot something moving around and realize it's a person. One wearing Birta's woolly hat.

'Stop, she's over there. I just saw her in her red coat. Let me go and get her; she's probably on her way to yours.'

He stops and I jump out. 'I'll bring her here, just a sec.' On impulse I run round to the driver's side, kiss his cheek through the window and leg it into the trees. 'Birta!'

She's about twenty feet away and turns immediately.

'Tanz! What are you doing here? I was on my way to see if you were home.'

I pick my way through the trees and she does the same towards me, until I'm breathing in the smoke and patchouli scent of her hair and neck as I give her a hug. Everything about her is so familiar, it makes me wonder about what Thor said about past-life stuff, or being separated from her when I was very young. There's a big rock just sitting there about five feet away, like it was placed there to rest on, and we settle down on it and Birta produces her trusty flask full of that special moss tea. She fills two tin cups.

'So, Tanz, I got the strongest feeling in the world I needed to see you. You weren't around last night so I thought I'd try again.'

'Yes, sorry about that. The most amazing thing happened . . .'

As I'm saying this, I'm starting to feel extremely strange. Surreal, like I just had too much caffeine (in my case that would take *a lot* of coffee). I look at Birta and her cheeks are glowing – not just rosy, glowing with life. Her eyes are so bright. And so fucking sad too. I didn't properly notice before, but the depth of those eyes is hard to take in. Something's happened, it's not just me that's had a revelation.

'What's going on, Birta?'

'What do you mean?' As she says it, she puts her hand on my neck, winding her fingers under my hair and hat, and stares at me levelly. Her hand isn't cold. Holding the tea must have warmed it. 'You're leaving, aren't you?'

'Yes, I'm flying home. My friend who books tours is sorting the flight for me. He's over there, waiting in the Jeep. He's like us, a wizard, he's not a shit. I think you'll love him. I want to send you a little pay-as-you-go mobile phone, via him, so I can call you. Would that be okay?'

She laughs. 'Extraordinary. What an incredible woman you are. You found the bones, you released her. I sense it. The Hidden Ones showed you the place, I think . . .'

I should have known she'd 'feel' it. Also, I should have known she knew more of the *Huldufólk* than she was letting on.

'Yes! We were led to them. Helene's with her son. And the bones will be officially "discovered" today. Buried close to the summer house.'

Birta's eyes fill with tears and a big one falls down her cheek. She still fixes a smile on her face, though. It makes my eyes fill too.

'Are you okay? What's wrong, Birta? Was it . . . ? Look, I know about the suicide. Was Kristin your mum? The one who had the affair with that murdering shit?'

Birta blinks away more tears, takes a sip of her tea.

'He wasn't a murdering shit to her. He was a charming, hard-working man who helped fix up her leaking house. Still leaking now, you saw it! She was such a lost woman in those days. Solitary and careful.'

Birta looks so hurt. What she must have been through with this knowledge on her shoulders. Did she tell anyone else or has she carried this heartache all on her own?

'She didn't account for this man showing up and kissing her so softly, Tanz. He was extremely mentally damaged, she could feel it, but also very tender with her. She poured love over him. She fed him her favourite recipes and held him, and drank with him, and spoke of the world with him and he opened up and told her he loved her, but that he'd done bad things. Told her that he was angry about so much. Told her that she made him feel like a whole person. He said all the things a man will say to a woman to make her feel like the only one, and she opened herself right up to it. He said he had a wife but it was platonic now, that it was over and that he wanted to start again, with his actual true love. They were going to visit Denmark together. Kristin loved the art and architecture there and he wanted to explore it with her. But then one day . . . like the dream you had . . . they were making love together, in absolute bliss, then there was this awful screaming. Helene had been watching them. The ecstasy turned to fear when his face changed and Kristin saw a side to him she'd never seen before. He roared like a demon as he pulled his clothes on. He told Kristin that his wife was mad, a raving lunatic, and he was going to send her home to England. But Kristin was no fool and his reaction had scared her. After he left she waited a little while, then jumped on her bicycle and went to the place she knew he was living. She'd not been there before, but it wasn't far and she needed to know what was going on. She hid behind an abandoned, broken tractor and watched him pull that poor, dead woman out of the house by the legs and put a blanket over her. Then he went back in and came back with a little boy. He was carrying a dead child, Tanz.'

Birta is fully crying now. I put my arms around her and she sobs into my coat.

'How could she live with that? How could anyone live with that? In her eyes she'd just caused a woman and child to be murdered. And she now knew the man she loved was a savage beast.'

'I'm so sorry, Birta. You don't have to talk any more. That poor lady.'

'No, I must finish. I'm so sorry I lied to you, didn't tell you I knew all of this. But it had to unfold naturally.'

'What happened to her?'

'She went to the road, and hitched a ride to Akranes. She was used to long hikes and it didn't take her very long to get up on the cliffs once she got there. Then she jumped. Nothing could have saved her, she jumped from so high. And she died feeling like she had killed Helene. Because she'd been a fool and believed a liar. Again.'

'I'm so sorry, Birta. That you've had to carry this. That your poor mum had to believe that she caused the deaths of Helene and Paul. She didn't. That man, Jack, he changed his name when he left here. He was seriously mentally ill and always in trouble. Died in a pub fight in the end. Even when he first came here, the police in England were after him for threatening another woman with an axe.'

She hangs her head. 'Such a bad man.'

'You shouldn't live your life cut off and hiding, Birta. I know men have upset you, but a lot of blokes are bloody idiots and you're a powerful witch. You probably scare them with your power; they probably adore you but can't handle your brilliance. I just wish I could tell Kristin that

Jack cried for her. Even years later. He told a stranger that she was his true love. Yes, what he did was evil, but he didn't lie when he said he loved her. That bit may have been twisted, but it was real.'

Birta takes a deep breath when I say this, then slowly, staring into my eyes with absolute warmth, she leans forward and kisses me on the mouth. Not sexual, not long, but intimate and loving. She drops her cup and removes mine too, makes me stand up with her, taking both my hands. I feel a rush of energy through her palms; it makes me dizzy. I have no idea what's going on.

'We are sisters, Tanz. Not in the domestic worldly sense. On the grandest of grand scales. You came here to set someone free, you felt her call, you knew what was needed, because that is your destiny. You know the call of your sisters and brothers, you always will. I have been so stuck, wandering and lonely. Now you've said the magic words and tied up the ends and I can be free. Go and get Thor. I'll wait here.'

This feels off, all of this feels off. I feel like my heart's breaking. Why am I so upset all at once?

'Go to Thor. Tell him that I, Kristin Birta Gunnarsdóttir, thank him for helping and understanding the amazing woman that stands before me. Love whoever you feel to love, Tanz. You are not ordinary; do what you need to do, and touch who you need to touch. I will see you again in the blink of an eye, my sister. Thank you for coming here. I love you.'

'Birta?'

'Tanz, what are you doing?' Thor is behind me, standing

by a rowan tree I didn't even notice, the berries shining red, even in the woody shadows. He looks freaked out and his loud shout makes me jump.

'Thor, this is . . .' I turn back to Birta. She's gone. No cups, bag, flask, nothing. Gone. I have no fucking idea what's going on. I look back at Thor.

He cocks his head. 'You were talking to thin air.'

'What?'

'You were sitting on that rock, then standing with your hands out, talking to thin air.'

'Noooooooo. No, no, no, noooo.' I can't breathe. I can't breathe and I won't believe this. I start to hyperventilate. Thor runs and catches me as I pitch forward. She's my friend. She felt as real as anyone and she smelled like home. And she was here seconds ago. How can she just disappear? I fall heavily onto the ground and Thor wraps himself around me as I sob my heart out, pulling in ragged gasps of air.

'Tanz, what happened? What going on?'

'My friend. My beautiful friend. She's not here. She died, all that time ago. She jumped off a fucking cliff. I can't bear it.'

My tears are like Gullfoss Falls: heavy and they just keep coming. Thor doesn't ask anything else, just holds me, my devastation taking even me by surprise. Kristin Birta Gunnarsdóttir. She gave me her middle name. And it wasn't Helene who called me here, it was her. She helped Helene to find her peace, through me. My amazing new friend; I was going to make her have a phone so I could call her and talk to her about spooky stuff, I was going to visit her another time and buy some of her pottery and make her stay with me in town and come for rhubarb mojitos. I was going to show off to everyone I knew that I had a sassy Icelandic witch as a mate. But no, she died long ago. A beautiful magical soul in limbo, wandering round the Icelandic wilderness, unable to leave until she knew Helene was okay and reunited with her son. Her guilt was so misplaced. I stop crying and wipe my face on my sleeve. I must look like a wet, mushy beetroot right now. Thor seems crestfallen.

'Are you okay?'

'I don't know what I am. Birta was Kristin. She's dead.'

'I guessed it when I saw you talking to nobody. I'm so sorry.'

The yearning that wells up in me is almost too much.

'Can we just drive further up for a minute, look at where she lived?'

When we get past the trees, there's a modern cabin there, built from the ruin of a stone dwelling, some of the stone walls still intact, but with a wood and glass extension. And there's no one there. It's definitely closed up for winter. Thor stops the Jeep and I just sit and stare and wonder if I'm mad.

'This is where it was. It's not here now. How could this happen? I mean, it was all as solid as real life. And I hugged her and smelled her. She was real. Am I bloody mad?'

'No. You're just special.'

'I don't want to be special. I don't want to make friends with people then find out they don't exist any more, that they died horribly and there's nothing I can do for them.

I don't want to discover where I visited was a mirage and everything that happened wasn't real. Everyone will think I'm a loon. And I'm fucking heartbroken, Thor. *My heart . . . !*'

He leans over from the driver's seat and holds me as everything starts to go black. What the hell is wrong with me?

SEX MAGIC

I wake up in the bedroom upstairs. The wood burner is lit and I'm under the covers in my clothes. There are voices outside, the sky is darkening and I have no idea how long I've been asleep. I'm so exhausted I can't find it in me to look for my phone. There's water on the table at the side of the bed and lifting my arm to get the glass and take a sip is as much as I can manage. I can't cope with the Birta thing. For the most part, I can take anything, even a raging man with a knife trying to end my life, but this has taken me to the next level of 'nope'. I begin to whimper when it hits me again, that my poor friend isn't on this planet any more because she jumped off a cliff in 1976. It's just too much.

I close my eyes. I want to fall asleep. I want to forget this horrible thing. I'm done with being a spooky woman, I can't take pain like this. Just as I'm sinking into the abyss, I hear a voice from the end of the bed.

'*Chosen.*'

I know who it is, of course I do. I try to open my eyes

but it's not happening. I'm paralysed but I don't actually care. Anything to escape this hurt. His voice gets closer and suddenly he's by my ear. He places a hand on my forehead, his touch like feathers.

'*The lessons aren't easy but you can take them.*'

'I can't bear it, Alfvin. I'm just a lass from Gateshead trying to live my life. I'm not equipped for all of this death and weirdness.'

The smell of the room changes as I lie here. Now there is a crackling fire nearby and there are echoes. We are in the bedroom but we're somewhere else too, a cave. It's the most discombobulating feeling but also perfectly in line with the situation. Two places at once is exactly right.

'*You are guided. Always. Birta brought you here. She protected this room for you so you would feel safe. She could not help Helene, they were in different realms. You gave them both release. Rejoice.*'

'I will. When I stop crying.'

He gives that 'cough, cough' noise that signals amusement.

'Alfvin, what are you? You're not a fucking elf, that's for sure.'

There's another 'cough, cough'.

'*A guide, a healing angel, a spirit helper. The voice inside. The knowing heart. There are realms for all "others". We are "other" but we are also here. That is what I am. Two realms, one spirit.*'

He says this close to my ear and I feel a tingle in my forehead.

'I love that. I love that you've helped me. But how are you linked to Birta?'

'She jumped from the rocks. We live in the rocks. We watched the breath leave her body. Her spirit was not like others. So we watched and guarded her while she wandered and gathered strength. Like the bones buried in our land. We watched and waited and then Birta found you. Your spirit had grown, aligned with hers. Sisters. She called you across the miles and you came. True kinship.'

'Wow. So it wasn't because I'm a lovesick idiot after all.'

'That man was a vessel. Not worthy of more. Do not think of him again. What you need is always sent.'

'I'm so fickle with men.'

'No. Do not stay with one mate until you meet your match. Until then, sex magic. It will present itself and it will help.'

'What, so be a slut?'

'Sex magic. Healing. You will always know.'

I actually like the sound of sex magic, though I still don't know what it means exactly. What I do know is that as he says this, something relaxes inside me, a knot in my belly loosens. A worry that I'm a bad person for going off people or not wanting to settle yet, for choosing 'wrong' ones, for needing excitement. Maybe it's all part of a process, a process that takes time and is still unravelling.

'Alfvin?'

'Yes.'

'When I leave Iceland, do I lose you?'

'No. All is connected.'

That's a bit too cryptic for me but I think it's the best I'm going to get.

'I think I'm going to cry again.'

His hand covers my eyes and he whispers something in an ancient language I don't understand. Then he leans as close to my ear as possible and I feel the tiniest whisper of breath.

'*Joy after pain. Peace be to you, Chosen.*'

His presence is suddenly gone. I open my eyes and blink, realizing that the noise from outside has abated. Car doors are closing and vehicles driving off. Soon after, Thor gently enters the room with a tray with bread and cheese on it, plus a tumbler of red wine. In the light from the burner, his face is a mask of kindness and care. He sits at the side of the bed and I reach my hand from under the covers to hold his.

'How are you feeling, my tired little witch?'

'A bit stupid. Did I faint?'

'I think it just all got too much. Understandably. You suddenly just faded away.'

'Hand me that drink, please.' I struggle a little more upright and take a sip, then another.

'The police have gone, for now. As has Ernest. They're all a bit confused. They had no idea anyone had even died. It was so long ago.'

'I think we're all a bit confused, Thor. Come here.'

He climbs onto the bed as I shrug off my jumper, leaving me in just a vest. He goes to hug me but I lean back and look him in his deep, kind, wizard eyes.

'Kiss me.'

He hesitates momentarily, probably scared, but he doesn't have to be asked twice. And as he brushes his fingertips down the bare skin of my arm, I feel goose bumps that aren't to do with the cold. His kiss is soft and the energy between us is unhurried but electric. We drink each other in and suddenly I'm as hungry for Thor as I've ever been for anyone in my whole life. We have shared experiences in a short time that others couldn't even comprehend, and I know he is a respectful man but I need that wall to come down right now. I need to meet him in that private space where nothing is hidden. I help him undress and get under the covers and he does the same for me, and all of the sadness, intensity, exhilaration and inexplicable insanity of the past week takes over and the kissing becomes frantic and we're carried away to a place with no inhibition and no time.

Okay, so this is what Alfvin may have meant by sex magic. It certainly feels pretty magical. Every time. All night.

DEPARTURE

I'm in the departure lounge at Keflavík airport and facing the music from everyone I didn't call for four days. Luckily my cat-sitter, Steve, got my text and was fine with it. Inka's as much his cat as mine these days. But I've called my mam and she's not happy at all.

'What the hell are you doing in Iceland? Your great-auntie Jean was a lunatic, you know! You're not going loopy, are you?'

'MAM! No, I just wanted to write something and someone offered me a free place to work, so I jumped at it.'

'I thought you were in trouble! You could have been murdered, you always seem to be up to your neck in murderers and knives these days.'

'It's not "always", Mam, it's just that I've been a bit unfortunate with a couple of investigations.'

'Well, all I can tell you is I nearly called the police, but then I had a dream and this nice lass with long hair, reddish-blonde like your auntie Paula's, she said, "Oh, she's helping me, she's fine."'

I can't speak for a moment as this gets me right in the throat.

'Tanz, did you hear me? She said you were sisters. She was a good lass. Put my mind at rest. But you're lucky, I nearly reported you missing.'

'Thank you, Mam.'

'What?'

'Thank you. You're very clever.'

'Eeeeeeee, well, I've not been called clever before.'

'You are. You're amazing.'

'You are going loopy, aren't you?'

I can't help laughing at this.

'Maybe I am, Mam.'

'Well, anyway, safe flight. Ring me at the other end. And be careful of that Icelandic lot, I was reading about them in the paper. They believe in elves, you know?' She begins to chortle down the phone. 'Maybe that's why you went there, they're as loopy as you.'

'Bye, Mam, speak to you later.'

'Bye, pet.'

I can hardly believe I'm flying home. This is the most intense experience I've had to date, and that's saying something. Thor left me at the departure gate, and it's safe to say we both felt like changed people. Our hug was like a goodbye to a piece of my soul. I know when I take off part of me will be left here, among the mossy rocks, in Thor's summer house and on Mount Esja, the female volcano with a beating heart.

But I also know that a hot shower without the smell of eggs, a cuddle with my probably very in-a-huff cat

Inka and a night in a starfish shape in my own bed will cure a lot of ills. Intense experiences need to be balanced out with humdrum normality or it all just gets to be too much. I have no concrete thoughts right now about what's gone on or what just happened with Thor or the wonder of Alfvin. That will all have to be stored temporarily and processed later. Right now I think a flute of cold fizz and jotting some stuff down in my new notebook might be in order. I'm certainly not short of material to write about. I'm probably now a leading world expert in being haunted by people nobody knew were dead, and in losing my new female friends in the most traumatic ways possible. I raise my glass to Birta as I sit at a little table next to the chiller cabinet, which is filled with open salmon and dill sandwiches. And write my first line:

It all started with Abba and a bloody scary power cut . . .

EPILOGUE

The flight is just skimming Scotland when a familiar voice pipes up.

'Well, that was interesting.'

Frank. He's in my bad books.

'Oh, hello, Scarlet Pimpernel. Yes, it was interesting, and really intense, and you were very notable by your absence. Thank you very much.'

'You didn't need my help from where I was looking. You had a witch sister, an elf and a ginger Viking who thinks you're a goddess.'

'I am a goddess, and Alfvin is not a fucking ELF.'

'Whatever. Just to let you know there's something going on that you're going to have to help with when you get back. Spookiness galore. You need a night in your own bed first, then I think shit might start hitting the fan.'

'Frank! I need a rest, it's all been so intense.'

'Exactly. A few nights at home, and then you'll be ready.'

'At least give me a clue.'

He's bloody gone. Of course he has. Just to think I was

in a strange bed yesterday convinced I never wanted anything to do with spooky stuff ever again, and here I am already getting intel from my dead mate on my next 'case'. If that's what you call it.

It's going to be very strange not cuddling up with Thor tonight. How weird that I was on a plane heading to Iceland obsessed with another man. Now he's just a dick and I've been restored by someone I knew nothing about until I landed there.

I close my eyes and, as I do, I hear the tiny tinkling of a bell. The bell around my neck that I will keep in a special box once I'm back in London, because it's too precious to lose. It tinkles again. Actually, that isn't 'my' bell. I haven't moved a muscle. My breath catches as I suddenly feel an energy close by that I'd know anywhere, an empty fullness, two things at once. Then I hear a whisper close to my ear.

'*Chosen. A gift.*'

Just then the Icelandic stewardess approaches. She's carrying a square thing wrapped in brown paper.

'Hello. I hope you don't mind, I'm a friend of Thor. He said he had a gift for you, but to wait 'til you were nearly home.'

She's blonde with china-blue eyes.

I laugh. 'Wow, Thor knows everyone.'

Her accent is so pretty, like her eyes. 'Yes, he does. And I wouldn't do this for everyone but he said it was very important.'

I take the package and pull off the paper. It's a small canvas. I know the sofa I'm seeing, a fire is burning and a woman is asleep curled up. That's me on Birta's sofa. The colours are darkened, like it was painted by candlelight. I know I woke up on this settee feeling like time had stood still, with a loud clock ticking. Someone obviously watched me while I was sparko. There's a note with the picture.

Tanz. This was one of the artworks they found in the barn when Kristin killed herself in 1976. I spoke to the owner. They stored them in the loft in a local gallery and let me buy this. I think they were scared her paintings were cursed. Of course they weren't, this was waiting for you and they let me buy it cheap. I hope you love it like I love you. Thor x

My heart explodes. Proof. This wouldn't prove anything to anyone else, but it shows that Birta and I shared the time I hoped we did, it wasn't a dream. And as for Thor . . . Well, I don't even know how to start processing that. Love. What a funny thing.

ACKNOWLEDGEMENTS

As always, I'd like to thank everyone at Pan Macmillan for being amazing. Kinza, my fabulous editor; Lucy Hale, Empress Queen of the Universe; Rosa, Mia and everyone else involved with my books, from finance, to marketing, to audio, to cover design. The team are incredible, and I'm so lucky.

I'd also like to thank some people who just make life better. Thank you to my son, Flynn, for being a legend. Thank you Ruth and Megan for the magic, the whistling and the 'om's in the woods. Thank you Katya for being a one-off, shiny diamond made of generosity. Thank you Doon and Kricka for always showing up and being wonderful mates. Thank you Verity for having the best music taste in the world except for me.

Thank you Erin, Mandasue, Ali Lee and all my witch sisters for lending me your ears and your sorcery. Thank you Lee and Rich for lovely chats, lovely dinner and inviting me to your amazing time-slip cottage. Thank you to all my Good Rooms chums and Avenue Mews stunners for saving my sanity. Thank you Katie G for your kindness, Kitty for your wisdom, Anna Quinn for your unwavering support and all my lasses, far and wide, for your strength and brilliance. Thank you to the talented Adrian Cecil for being 'my people'. And, last but never least, thank you Cedric for the warm scarf around my neck when my heart was frozen, plus the much-needed hugs and music chats. All love.

WHEN THE DEAD CALL . . .

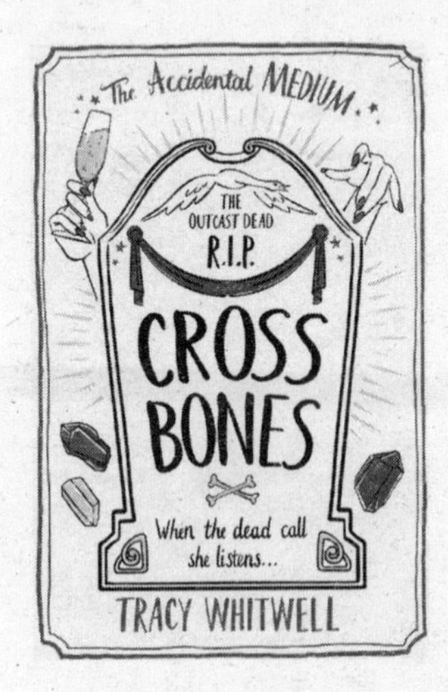

Discover the full Accidental Medium series!